"There are millions of clocks in the world.

Let Mr. Westerfield and others find some at yard sales."

"That's what I'm trying to say, Connie. There are millions of clocks for you to choose from, also. Maybe you should let the man have it, and you find something else when the time and money is right."

She must've had a horrible look on her face, for he quickly backpedaled, offered a hasty good-bye, and headed for the door.

Connie inhaled a deep breath to calm herself. Why was this happening to her? After cleaning up, she plopped down on the sofa to stare at the clock. Why, out of all the clocks in this world, did this one have to mean so much to Silas Westerfield? And now even strangers were going to bat for him. She tried to consider this from the older man's viewpoint but couldn't. The man was obviously a dealer who found something at a yard sale that caught his eye, and she had snatched it away. Wasn't there a saying for such things? Finders keepers, losers weepers?

She sat mulling over it all—Silas Westerfield, Donna, and finally Lance. She was certain Lance entered his opinion out of a concern for her financial status. He had seen the empty fridge. He thought it would do her wallet good to sell the clock and look for another. He wanted what was best for her. Perhaps the conversation showed that Lance truly cared about her.

Connie gazed at her purchase. Little did he realize, but what was best for her right now was this clock. It brought her companionship and a wealth of fond memories from days gone by. If only she didn't feel so troubled. Instead of joy, she now wrestled with confusion. *God*, she prayed, *help me sort this all out, somehow, someway.*

LAURALEE BLISS, a former nurse, is a prolific writer of inspirational fiction as well as a home educator. She resides with her family near Charlottesville, Virginia, in the foothills of the Blue Ridge Mountains—a place of inspiration for many of her contemporary and historical novels. Lauralee Bliss writes inspirational fiction to provide readers with entertaining stories, intertwined with Christian principles to assist them in their day-to-day walk with the Lord. Aside from writing, she enjoys gardening, cross-stitching, reading, roaming yard sales, and traveling. Lauralee invites you to visit her website at www.lauraleebliss.com.

Books by Lauralee Bliss

HEARTSONG PRESENTS

Don't miss out on any of our super romances. Write to us at the following address for information on our newest releases and club information.

Heartsong Presents Readers' Service
PO Box 719
Uhrichsville, OH 44683

Or visit www.heartsongpresents.com

Time
Will Tell

Lauralee Bliss

Heartsong Presents

To my beloved grandmothers: Grandma Schreiber for her old cuckoo clock, the princess glass shoe, and the candy dish. In memory of Grandma Braun for her delicious kuchen and the fascinating laundry chute.

With thanks to:
Lorena Perez
Wanda Hume
The Clock Shop of Virginia
Charlottesville, Virginia

A note from the Author:
I love to hear from my readers! You may correspond with me by writing:

Lauralee Bliss
Author Relations
PO Box 719
Uhrichsville, OH 44683

ISBN 1-59310-259-3

TIME WILL TELL

Our mission is to publish and distribute inspirational products offering exceptional value and biblical encouragement to the masses.

PRINTED IN THE U.S.A.

Or check out our Web site at www.heartsongpresents.com

one

BUZZ.

Not again. Connie jumped out of the shower at the sound, racing to switch off the alarm clock at her bedside. A pattern of water droplets decorated the carpet below her feet. She never remembered to turn off the alarm come Saturday morning. Her internal clock worked beautifully every weekend, awakening her to a picture-perfect day filled with the hope of finding treasures at the yard sales she planned to attend.

Friday nights were spent scanning the newspaper, circling the yard sale ads that interested her. On a map, she starred in pencil the streets holding the sales. This Saturday, to her delight, she found a moving sale right down the street from where she lived. Many times she'd had to drive long distances to find one that appealed to her. This sale in particular—held by her neighbor, Mrs. Rowe—tickled her interest. In the ad Mrs. Rowe cited several antique treasures and old books.

Connie rubbed the towel over her shoulder-length dark brown hair while scanning shelves of books purchased at previous yard sales. Half the books she owned were juvenile in nature. Connie often wondered why as a young, single woman she bothered buying children's books. Perhaps that maternal instinct was on the rise, or maybe it was the plain nostalgia of owning children's classics that had entertained her as a youngster.

Connie blow-dried her hair and quickly dressed. With the

5

sale just down the street, she hoped to be one of the first arrivals in her quest for a bargain. All around her apartment were telltale signs of previous yard sale finds—old plates, a small wooden table, a lamp, a painting of the ocean. . . Her wages from her job at the department store didn't quite cut it for her to be buying expensive possessions to fill her place. Instead she resorted to yard sales to find decorating ideas. A few of her coworkers went with her on her journeys Saturday mornings and were amazed at Connie's ability to sniff out obscure bargains. Soon they began giving Connie their lists and asking her to keep an eye out for items that would interest them. Connie was able to find an origami book for one worker's daughter, queen sheets in rose print, and even a crib for an expectant coworker. No doubt she could win Yard Sale Customer of the Year if such an award existed.

Connie quickly drank down a cup of coffee and ate a piece of toast spread with strawberry jam before heading out the door. No need for the car on this venture, with the first yard sale a mere five houses away. The clear blue sky slowly awakened with the first rays of morning sunlight. Birds chirped merrily from the trees as she hurried down the sidewalk. Neighbors' yards were all abloom in tulips and hyacinths. It was a perfect spring day.

Claudia Rowe was still dressed in her duster with a cloth turban wrapped around her head when Connie appeared in front of the house. Boxes were scattered on the lawn. The older woman stared at her in amazement before glancing at her watch.

"I don't open for another hour."

"I know," Connie said breathlessly. "I only live down the block. When I saw your ad, I knew this was the first place I wanted to look."

"You must be that young thing who lives in that apartment building down the street from me. I think I know everyone in this section of West Street. It will be hard for me to leave the neighborhood, but it's something I need to do."

Connie had never considered herself a "young thing," but she must seem young at twenty-five to someone over sixty. "I'm Connie Donovan. My coworkers call me the Yard Sale Queen."

"Really now. And why is that?"

"Because from March until August I'm at yard sales. I usually bring lists from others that tell me what to hunt for."

"Well, I suppose you can look around if you want. I'm going inside to get dressed. I'll be right back."

Connie smiled and began browsing. Most of the items for sale were typical of other yard sales she had been to—clothes, shoes, glassware, cookware, luggage pieces. . . There were a few toys and a box of books. Connie knelt down to sift through the books. She picked up a heavy hardcover with slick pictures of the nation's parks and sighed. How she would love to tour those parks one day. It reminded her of trips her family used to take every summer when she was young, traveling around in their old pop-up camper. She glanced around, reminiscing about it all, when a particular item caught her eye. She put down the book and picked up a clock that was sticking halfway out of a dusty box. It was no ordinary clock either, but an old-fashioned cuckoo clock. Connie looked at the carving of wood and the tiny door above the clock face where the little bird would pop out and call, *Cuckoo*. She was still examining it when Claudia Rowe appeared, carrying a cup of coffee.

"Isn't it a beautiful clock?" the older lady said with a sigh. "I've had it for many years."

"I suppose it works all right?"

"Of course. It cuckoos every half an hour. It requires winding every eight days by pulling the chains here. I've actually had it in storage a very long time. I felt with the move and all it was time to get rid of it. No sense keeping memories like that around anymore, especially when there's nothing left to hold on to."

Connie traced the polished wood with her fingers, noting the configuration of carved leaves and the profile of a bird etched into the top. A clock like this must be worth a fortune—far above her humble means. It was silly to even consider it.

"I really should have sold it in the paper," Claudia continued, "but I thought I would put it out and see if I had any takers. Besides, if you advertise something in the paper, you never know who will respond. I don't want strange people knowing my phone number and calling me up or coming inside my home."

"I don't blame you. You have to be careful nowadays." Connie continued to stare at it, thinking how much it reminded her of her grandmother's clock that once hung in the living room. After her grandmother passed away, Connie had tried desperately to find the old clock only to discover, like many of Grandma's possessions, it had been sold at auction. Now it seemed as if God had resurrected the clock from long ago. "How much do you want for it?"

"Well, I'm not really sure. I haven't thought about it, to be honest. But you seem like a nice young lady who would take care of it. I suppose you can have it for a hundred."

Connie gulped. The most she had ever spent at a yard sale was thirty, and that was after she'd managed to dicker on the price for the small wooden table now sitting in the foyer of her apartment. She glanced at the woman, wondering if she was in the bargaining mood this early in the game. "Would you take fifty?"

She shook her head. "I'm sorry, but I think a hundred is very generous. I know the clock doesn't mean anything to me now, but I am in the process of moving, and I need the money."

Connie sighed. She turned away and opened her wallet to find fifty dollars. In another part of her wallet she kept her gas money for the next two weeks. Pulling out the bills, she discovered she had seventy-five dollars but no more.

Claudia Rowe moved off to arrange some clothing on a table while Connie returned to the cuckoo clock. How much it reminded her of her grandmother's home and that time in her life. Tears filled her eyes just thinking about it. As a little girl, she could still see the rescue squad arriving to take her mother to the hospital after she fainted on the bathroom floor. When they said she'd suffered an aneurysm and might never wake up, Connie cried for hours. She refused all comfort, even from family members. The only comfort she found during those long days and nights spent in her grandmother's home was from the old-fashioned cuckoo clock hanging on the wall. The faithful bird popped out every half hour to greet her like a friend. Grandma would try to think of things to do while she and her younger brothers waited anxiously for word about their mother. But it was the cuckoo that Connie looked to time and time again until she was reunited with her mother.

Just then other customers began arriving for the sale— several women and then a man wearing a hat, bearing a distinct limp. Connie saw them edging toward the table where the precious cuckoo clock rested. Immediately she picked up the clock and approached the older neighbor. When Claudia hastily agreed to the seventy-five dollars, she handed over all the money in her wallet, including her gas money for the next two weeks. At that moment, she didn't care. In her eyes the clock was tantamount to finding a precious gem. When life brought troubles her way, she would look at the clock and remember God's faithfulness in bringing her through times of turmoil to a joyful end. It was just like the day her mother walked into Grandma's home after awakening from her weeklong coma. This clock was God's gift to her, a gift that symbolized a miracle and one she would treasure forever.

Arriving home, Connie immediately found a place on the wall of her living room to display the clock. She eagerly set and wound the clock. In no time the half hour passed and the door opened to reveal the cuckoo bird, ready for its first greeting in its new home. Connie couldn't help smiling. The clock had been worth its price, even if now she must scrimp to meet her needs. Maybe she could find some extra hours at work, like doing inventory, to cover the cost. She decided to call her friend, Donna, who'd worked the previous evening at the customer service desk. Maybe Donna knew if any extra hours were available on the monthly calendar.

"There must be a reason you're looking for work in inventory," Donna said with a chuckle. "What did you waste your money on this time?"

"You'll never guess."

"You're right, I won't. I never know what you'll come home with. Which reminds me, any luck at finding a nice-looking table lamp?"

"I only went to one yard sale today and ran out of money. So I came home."

"Wow. Must have been one terrific sale."

"It was." Connie inhaled a breath. "I got a clock."

"Did you say *a* clock? How much did you spend?"

"Seventy-five."

Connie could imagine Donna's "Are you kidding me?" expression as she asked, "Who would spend *all* her money on *one* clock?"

"It reminded me of being in my grandmother's house when I was little and the time my mom went to the hospital after a brain aneurysm burst. For days the only thing that comforted me was my grandmother's faithful cuckoo clock. It's symbolic, I guess; this clock reminds me that God took care of her. Mom not only survived, but she is healthy to this day."

Donna seemed disinterested. "Still, seventy-five bucks is quite a bit for just a clock," she finally said.

"Yes, if it was any old clock. But I'll tell you, it could be the twin to my grandmother's cuckoo clock. For all I know it might even *be* her clock. I mean, her things were sold off at auction. Maybe I should check with the lady down the street and see if that's where she got it. Wouldn't that be incredible?"

"Definitely not of this world," Donna agreed.

Connie was glad to hear this statement as she had been talking with her friend about the Lord. She didn't preach but rather shared with Donna the times in her life when she felt God was looking out for her interests. She hoped it might minister to her friend in some small way. Which reminded her, she needed to have Donna and some of her other women coworkers for lunch soon. Connie tried to have people over as often as she could. There was something about sharing meals together that brought people closer. Now if only there might be a love relationship in her life as well as good friendships. Not a day went by when she didn't dream about a man waltzing into her life and whisking her away to some island paradise. She sighed and gazed at the clock once more. God had His perfect timing as He did when He brought the beloved clock into her life. He would bring a man into it, too—at the right time and in the right place.

"Oh, and guess what the news is at work, Connie? We've got a new employee. And he is out of this world."

At the word "he," Connie listened more intently. Not that a guy at work would interest her all that much. Most of the men who worked at the store were stock boys earning money to put toward their college degrees and were much younger than she. The head manager was married. And mainly women worked as cashiers or manned the customer service counter.

"His name is Lance Adams. He's training to become part of the management team."

"That's nice."

"C'mon, Connie. I've seen goldfish show more enthusiasm."

"I'm hardly going to be enthusiastic about some guy who's probably married if not already attached. Besides, if he hates yard sales I'm fresh out of luck."

"You're too much. I'll try to discover his phone number and find out some other tidbits for you. Then maybe you'll feel more comfortable."

Warmth spread across Connie's face at the thought of Donna snooping into some stranger's life—and just for her benefit. She tried to tell Donna she wasn't interested, but something inside her held out a hope that perhaps this man was unattached and looking for someone like her.

Connie began considering her lifestyle and characteristics. Besides her love for the Lord and her interest in yard sales, there wasn't much else spectacular about her. She had shoulder-length dark brown hair parted down the middle, her mother's German nose, and her father's dark brown eyes and dark skin tone from his Hispanic ancestry. Many considered her job at the store on the low end of the employment scale. She had nothing of real value in her home but the sentimental value of the cuckoo clock she'd purchased today. Her clothes were ordinary jeans and tops, with a few pairs of slacks and blouses for the workday. She disliked buying clothes; consequently there was little hanging in her closet. She did love Christian music and would often listen to her favorite artists on the stereo. Occasionally she might play a multiplayer game on the Internet with her brother Louis. If Lance liked computer games, they might actually have something in common. Then she recalled her assumptions about the man—married or with a steady girl-friend who had a nice job, beautiful clothes, and a flashy smile. She might as well accept it. There was no hope.

"You haven't heard a word I've said, have you?"

Connie gulped, realizing she had no idea what Donna had been talking about.

"Don't worry," Donna continued good-naturedly. "I still plan to find out what I can about Lance. When can I come see your clock?"

"I'll have you over for lunch soon," Connie promised.

"Sounds good. See you Monday."

The phone clicked, precisely at the moment when the little bird popped out of the clock and began its merry serenade. Connie had to smile. At least she wouldn't be lonely tonight. God had provided her a feathered friend, even if it was made of wood. And maybe, just maybe, He might have others waiting in the wings, too.

two

"I hope you'll do the smart thing and sell that clock on the Internet."

Connie had just taken off her jacket and hung it in her locker when Donna bounced up behind her. It was Monday morning, a new start to the workweek, and already Donna was after her about her precious clock. "Of course not. I love it."

"Haven't you heard about these people who resell their stuff on the Internet and make tons of money? I know people who do it all the time."

Connie wished her friend would consider other things besides money. As it was, she would never dream of selling her sweet clock. She had just slipped her lunch bag into the small employee locker when Donna grabbed her arm.

"Look! Quick! Over there! Isn't he magnificent?"

Connie thought a movie star had suddenly graced the premises, ready to sign autographs with the way her coworker was reacting. Donna pointed to a tall man with dark hair who was chatting with several of the cashiers. All the young girls had dreamy looks, their fingers slowly pushing strands of hair behind their ears in shy displays.

"That's him. Lance Adams. Make your move."

"I'm not making any move," Connie told her tersely. Her hand shook as she shut the locker. "Whoever he is, he's obviously a womanizer. He has all the girls eating out of his hand."

"He's interacting with the employees, silly. And he's training for management. Lots of money—that is, after his training is complete. What a keeper."

Connie stole a glance at the new manager-in-training while his back was turned. He was tall in stature, with brown hair in a shade close to her own. He wore tailored slacks and a broadcloth shirt with a silk tie befitting his status. She shook her head. There was no possible way this man would give her the time of day, especially with the number of females working at the store. Ten to one was poor odds at best. And he was in management training, after all. Those in the upper echelon of the business world didn't associate with mere laborers. Connie adjusted the watchband on her wrist before tossing back her hair. There was only one thing she could do—concentrate on her work at customer service and forget about Lance Adams. As it was, she needed to check the schedule for some overtime so she could earn enough money to buy a tank of gas. *Either that or I'll have to drag out the old bicycle from storage.*

A young woman named Sally, with auburn hair and freckles, rushed up to her. "Oh, Connie, I just know you can get me out of my predicament. I need a rocking chair."

"A rocking chair!" Donna echoed with a laugh. "Aren't you a little young to be thinking about that?"

Connie cast her friend an irritated glance, wishing at times that Donna wasn't so blunt. She turned her attention to the young girl who smiled meekly. "You mean you want me to find you a rocking chair at a yard sale?"

"Everyone tells me how you can find the greatest deals at yard sales. All my mother does is reminisce about the rocker her grandmother once owned. I would like to get her one for her birthday."

This statement drew Connie's interest. "I'll have to tell you sometime about the wonderful cuckoo clock I just picked up on Saturday. My grandma had one almost exactly like it."

Sally grabbed her arm in excitement. "I just know you can find me a rocker, Connie. I'll pay you whatever it costs and even extra to cover your trouble."

"You don't need to do that."

"But I want to. The money's worth it. A rocker will absolutely make Mom's day, I just know it."

Connie smiled as Sally raced off to man her cash register, until she caught Lance Adams gazing in her direction. His dark eyes were large and luminous as they stared at her for a few seconds before turning to Mr. Drexer, the store manager. Connie wondered why he looked at her the way he did but pushed the thought aside to enter the customer service area. She sighed in dismay at the amount of garbage strewn across the desk—candy wrappers, coffee cups, papers with doodles on them. . . No doubt Donna had tried to keep herself awake Sunday evening while working overtime and hadn't bothered to clean up, leaving the mess to sit until Monday morning. All Connie needed was the new manager-in-training to see this sloppy workstation and get the wrong impression of her.

Connie had brought over the wastebasket, ready to toss out the trash, when suddenly his face peered over the counter. She dropped the wastebasket on the ground, dumping out the trash that included a half-filled can of soda. A brown stream trickled across the shiny linoleum.

"Oh!" she cried, glancing around for something to clean up the mess.

"Not a good way to start a Monday morning," Lance Adams observed.

Connie looked beyond him, thankful Mr. Drexer wasn't there, or he would have surely reprimanded her even though she was innocent. "Please believe me, I didn't make this mess."

"I'm sure you didn't." He reached out his hand. "Just wanted to introduce myself. Lance Adams."

Connie offered her hand in return only to find she was still clutching a chocolate wrapper, one she'd retrieved from the litter-strewn desktop. She tucked away the offending hand and offered him the other one. "Connie Ortiz."

"Ortiz. Is your family from Mexico?"

"No, we're not from Mexico," she retorted, a bit miffed. People were forever asking her this question. "My father's relatives are from Guatemala. And my favorite food isn't enchiladas either. Actually, I prefer a good Mediterranean pizza, the kind with prosciutto, black olives, and artichokes. Luigi's makes the best."

Lance blinked in surprise before offering a smile. "Sounds terrific. We should go there sometime."

Connie gaped at him in astonishment. Her hands began to shake at the mere thought of the man offering the semblance of a date—and when she didn't even know him. He must be more of a womanizer than she'd thought. She turned back to see the river of soda creeping toward her shoe. "Excuse me, but I have a mess here to clean up."

Instead of moving away, Lance came behind the customer service desk to see the garbage on the desk and the soda adding a distinctive pattern to the floor tiles. He grabbed up the phone and paged the janitor. "You'll be cleaned up here in no time. So tell me, do you have any concerns you'd like to discuss with regards to customer service?"

"Yes, as a matter of fact. Half the time the register here

doesn't work. We've never had enough pens. And we could use another employee for the evening hours, except that I need the job."

His eyebrow rose. "You already have a job."

Connie was becoming more and more flustered by this conversation. If only the man hadn't suggested the idea of going out for pizza. The statement had totally wrecked her nerves. Maybe Donna had tickled his ear about her. Then again, maybe he was just a nice guy looking to have everyone in the store love him. Perhaps he offered pizza outings to all the girls on the staff. Maybe he should throw them all one big pizza party and be done with it. "What I mean is, if we did hire another clerk, I wouldn't be able to pick up overtime, which I could really use right now."

"Money's that tight?"

Connie said little else about the money angle, nor did she mention her prized find at the yard sale that led to her poor financial status for the coming week. Instead she told him how an extra paycheck was always nice as she cleared the workstation of wrappers and stray paper.

"I'll see to your other requests—the extra pens and a technician to look at the cash register. Nice meeting you." He turned to greet other employees but not before offering her a wink.

Connie watched him interact with several women at the main cash registers, giving them each a friendly greeting and a handshake. The women reacted with smiles and wide eyes that scanned him in curiosity. With his winning personality, no wonder he was picked to be an assistant manager. She could see his lips move as he spoke, probably trying his pizza ploy on the others. Connie shoved a strand of hair behind one ear while mopping up the spilled soda since the janitor had failed to appear. There was no sense in being disappointed over the encounter. She knew all along this was too good to be true, though inwardly she wished Donna hadn't planted so many hopeful seeds.

Connie had just gotten her act together at the service counter when her first customer arrived, a young woman returning several articles of clothing. She went about her daily work and soon forgot the encounter with Lance. The day became busy, with the line for refunds and exchanges growing before her. She looked around for Donna in the hopes she could help out, but realized she had likely been snagged to do inventory as it was nearing the end of the month. The people in line grew antsy. Some began to sigh loudly and stare at their watches.

Suddenly the cash register jammed. Connie's face grew hot as she tried to make the system work, only to find it had frozen.

"What's the holdup here?" snarled a man with a balding head, waving a wrinkled shirt. "I only wanted to return this measly shirt, and I've been waiting here thirty minutes."

"I'm sorry, but it seems the cash registers are down."

The man swore before turning to the other customers in line. He began ranting about the incompetence of the employees while they chattered on the phone to their boyfriends. He continued on with his plan to take his shopping needs elsewhere, even if this was the only major store in the area. "And I hope you go out of business," he redirected toward Connie.

Connie bit her lip while trying to maintain her composure enough to page maintenance. When she failed to receive an answer to her call, she tried once more. This time, her shaky voice echoed over the store's loudspeaker. "Stan Harrison, will you please come to customer service? Stan Harrison?"

Several of the customers began drifting away until only the bald-headed man and one other lady stood before the counter. Again the man used choice words that nearly curled Connie's hair. This is what she hated most about her job, dealing with irate customers who blamed her for things totally out of her control. If only she could get the cash register to open.

Just then Lance Adams appeared, along with Stan who jiggled a set of tools. She breathed a sigh of relief, but not before the bald-headed man called her a name that mocked her Hispanic heritage. He then told her to go back to Mexico where she belonged. Connie nearly fainted on the floor.

"Excuse me, but that wasn't necessary," Lance told the man directly. "If you need assistance, I'll gladly take care of it. But don't harass my employees."

"I've been waiting here over an hour to return this thing," he barked before tossing the article of clothing into Lance's hands. "You can keep it and your store. I'm never coming here again."

Connie stood there, stunned by the encounter. Never in her life had anyone said such things to her. Of course she had heard stories from her father and how he was ridiculed for his heritage, but never once did she think it would happen to her.

"It looks like you could use a break," Lance whispered to her. "I'll get Donna to cover."

Connie nodded, unable to speak after the incident. She managed to walk to the lounge, her mind in a fog. She wished now she hadn't ignored Papa when he spoke of the old days and what happened to him as a young immigrant to the United States. To her they were just tales told for effect. She was an American, after all, even if she was born to a Hispanic father and a German mother. But little did she realize she carried within her a heritage that had suddenly been attacked when she least expected it.

"I'm sorry that happened," a soft voice directed her way. Connie glanced up to see that Lance had followed her into the lounge. He went and poured her a cup of coffee. "You take sugar?"

"One packet of the fake stuff. And a little milk." She threw herself onto the sofa. "I've never had that happen before. Papa told me how he was teased in school, especially over his accent. He kept bringing it up like it was the worst thing he had ever been through. I just ignored it. Now I wish I hadn't. It's like I ridiculed him, too, by refusing to listen."

Lance handed her the coffee. "Don't be so hard on yourself. That customer was completely out of line. And you did warn me about the cash register. I should have had someone look at it right away. I let you down, Miss Ortiz."

Connie blinked in surprise at this statement before taking a sip of her coffee. There were interesting features about this man named Lance Adams. He wasn't just a typical manager; he had a merciful heart for others. He sat down in another chair.

"Please call me Connie. Ortiz makes me sound like a brand of tortilla chip." Lance laughed even though Connie shook her head. "There I go again. Really, I do like my name and my heritage. I guess I just don't want to make a big deal out of it. But my eyes were sure opened today to some of the hate that's out there."

"It's hard when people become that way. Sometimes I don't understand why God would have us love people like that, but He does. And yes, He loves that man, too. Are you a church-goer by any chance?"

Connie nodded and described the community church she attended, only to see Lance's dark eyes widen. A smile erupted on his face.

"Would you believe, that's where I go, too?"

Connie stared in astonishment. She tried to picture the man among the members of the congregation but couldn't place him. As it was, the church had grown quite a bit over the last few months. Connie wasn't very good at introducing herself to strangers. She had a group of women she liked to sit with and paid little attention to others.

"Then we do understand the same language when it comes to dealing with irate people."

"If you mean we should be dumping coals on their heads, I guess so. Though I don't think that customer's scalp could get much redder. He looked boiling mad," she said.

Again Lance chuckled with warmth that made her feel good inside. It was almost as if she had known him for years rather than having just met him this morning. There was a friendliness about him that put her completely at ease. He sympathized with her struggles, and he had already helped her out of several predicaments. Maybe God had divinely set all of this up—first with Donna and then through the actions of the irate customer. Perhaps He was working to bring them together for some special purpose. She would then have two delightful gifts to call her own, the adorable cuckoo clock and handsome Lance Adams.

"It's hard keeping your cool in these kinds of situations,"

Lance agreed. "I've already found myself dealing with interesting situations here at the store, and I only began a few days ago. But I did work at another giant store, so dealing with problems comes naturally."

"You seem at home here," Connie agreed. She wanted to add that she was glad he had switched jobs and decided to grace their humble store with his presence but kept such comments to herself. Instead she answered his questions about church and some of the activities she was involved in. With that, Connie began sharing her yard sale experiences, deciding she might as well spill the beans about her interests. He said little about it and asked about some of the items she had purchased in the past. When she mentioned the precious cuckoo clock, Lance straightened and inquired where she bought it.

"My neighbor down the street. She's moving, so I guess she wanted to get rid of it. I did an Internet search and found that cuckoo clocks can cost several hundred to several thousand dollars. I really got a bargain."

"I guess so." Lance glanced at his watch. "Time to get back to work." He stood to his feet and opened the door of the lounge for her.

"Thanks again for coming to my rescue," she said, then caught herself when she realized what had come out of her mouth.

"Don't mention it. If you have any other trouble, call me on my pager. That's the quickest way you can get ahold of me." He gave her his business card before striding away to greet several people. Connie glanced down at the card he gave her with his name inscribed on it. Lance Edward Adams. The name sent tingles shooting straight through her. Lance Edward

Adams, her benefactor, her rescuer—the one who pledged to share her favorite pizza one day soon. She floated on a cloud of emotion to the customer service counter where Donna gave her a curious look.

"I see it's working out well," she said with a grin.

Connie squeezed the card Lance had given her. "You were right, old buddy, old pal. I'll treat you to an ice cream sundae after work. Oops, I don't have any money right now. I'll have to give you a rain check."

Donna laughed loudly, drawing the attention of several customers who again began to congregate in front of the counter, looking to bring back returns. "Connie, love will do wonders in your life."

With the warm, fuzzy feelings floating through her at that moment, Connie couldn't help agreeing.

three

Connie found it difficult concentrating at work after the encounter with Lance, though she rarely spoke to him for the remainder of the week. The way he helped her early on, especially when confronting the irate customer, remained in the forefront of her thoughts. She'd never met a man quite like him. On occasion, her brothers would stick up for her when confronting the neighborhood bully. Louis even took a punch in the lip to ward off such an attack. But the idea of an almost perfect stranger coming to her aid gave her a feeling of worth and confidence. The incident with the customer no longer affected her when she considered how Lance supported her. And from the conversations with other employees, compassion seemed to be his trademark. Mr. Drexer must be thrilled to have someone like Lance on the management team.

At the business meetings, the head manager often encouraged the employees to act like a family and be neighborly to one another. Lance exemplified the role to a tee. He was like a father, nurturing them, helping them out of difficulties that would creep up during the cycle of a normal workday. After the first week at his new job, Connie learned of at least ten different episodes where Lance was required to help a customer or an employee out of a jam. Surely he was a blessing in disguise.

Connie began a tally of the day's refunds before leaving the customer service counter to Freda, a young girl who worked the evening shift. Looking at the schedule, she was pleased to see that Freda was only working three days next week. Hopefully Connie could snag one or two of the days and make up for the money spent on the clock. She quickly jotted down her name and the hours she would work before forwarding the slip to personnel for approval. With a nod, Connie hastened to her locker to grab her purse.

"A great week so far, eh?" Donna asked with a wink.

"It started out a little strange, but yes, it's ending on a higher note."

"I was telling Lance all about you when I saw him earlier today," Donna said, taking out her own large black handbag from the locker. She rummaged for a tube of lipstick.

"You didn't."

"Of course I did. I told him how we were friends and how I knew all kinds of secrets about you." Donna traced some color on her lips before casting Connie a grin. "Just kidding. I did tell him, though, about your yard sale adventures. I must say he seemed very interested about that ridiculous clock you bought last Saturday."

"Maybe he likes antiques," Connie mused. *Wouldn't that be a catch—to find a guy who actually liked yard sales?* It seemed too good to be true. She could imagine getting together with Lance one fine Saturday morning. She would come equipped with the Saturday morning paper and the sales circled while Lance would provide the street map. Together they would drive around in his sports car searching for sales. He would follow her as she explained about the bargains to be had, even buying her a pretty vase in which to place a bouquet of red roses—

"Or maybe he likes the person who buys the antiques,"

Donna said, interrupting her thoughts. "He did ask why you like to buy other people's junk. I wasn't sure what to say, but he really answered his own question. He said, and this is what I loved, 'Connie must be someone who can take another person's junk and make it beautiful. It takes a special person to do that.' Isn't that just the sweetest thing you've ever heard? What a guy. If you let him go, honey, you might as well give up on life altogether."

Connie couldn't believe her ears after hearing this news. She said good-bye to Donna and headed for her car, all the while thinking about Lance's words. She wondered after Monday's mess at the customer desk, the scene with the customer, and then stories of her sales, whether Lance had already made up his mind about her. Could it be she had found her match in life and so soon? It seemed unreal. Yes, she had a nice conversation with him, and he had said some sweet things, but they'd just met. She needed to take this one step at a time and not rush it, even if everything was looking good. Connie knew that many times what seemed right could turn out wrong. And she didn't want to be wrong about Lance Adams, even if he was turning her heart topsy-turvy at the moment.

Connie stopped at a small grocery store on her way home. With the ten-dollar bill she had found in a desk drawer last evening, she bought some apple juice on sale, corn tortillas, cheese, a bunch of bananas, a head of lettuce, and some ground beef. She hoped the meat would last all next week if she divided it up into sandwich bags to put in the freezer. At the cash register, the amount came to $10.23. Connie paled as she scrambled to search in the bottom of her purse for the coins, only coming up with a dime. Behind her, the customers were growing irate. *Doesn't anyone have an ounce of patience while waiting in line?* Finally she took off one banana from the bunch, had it reweighed, and found the amount totaled exactly ten dollars.

Red-hot with embarrassment over the incident, Connie quickly made her way to the car, setting the plastic bags on the backseat before flinging herself into the driver's seat. She resisted shedding a tear over the incident but scolded herself for buying the dumb clock. Donna was right. She had no business making a purchase she couldn't afford right now. Her parents would have a fit if they found out how she was scrimping on food this month. Papa loved the huge meals Mom always fixed. If they found out that she only had a small tortilla with cheese, meat, and lettuce for dinner each day, they would make her pack up and move home.

Connie bit her lip and started the engine. No, she must have faith in all this. God would provide. If He fed the sparrows, He would feed her. His Word promised not to worry about food and clothing if she trusted Him. She lifted her head higher and headed home, feeling better after the incident that marred an otherwise upbeat day. Then she thought of Lance. What would he think if he found out she was as poor as a church mouse? Would he think she only liked him because of the money he made as an assistant manager? She shook her head. Lance appeared as genuine as could be, without giving a thought to another person's status. Besides the fact, he was a Christian with a servant's heart. She truly believed if God meant for she and Lance to be together, then it would work out somehow, someway.

When she neared her home, Connie found a stranger pacing back and forth before the door of her apartment. Despite the warmth of the spring afternoon, he wore a pale brown trench coat that came past his knees, along with a dark hat. He might have been a twin of Sherlock Holmes, except he walked with a distinct limp. After a time of pacing, he slowly eased himself down to sit on her doorstep.

Connie drove past the apartment and down the street, taking a good look at the man as she did. She then paused in front of Claudia Rowe's house, the same place where she purchased the cuckoo clock, and sat behind the wheel. What should she do? Obviously the man was waiting for her. She couldn't imagine why. Maybe he was an undercover cop or detective of some sort. A chill raced through her. Could something have happened to a family member? The mere thought made her quiver with anxiety. She saw the news each night on her little portable television. Pictures of lost family members or those involved in some type of crime flashed in her brain. But the man appeared a bit too feeble to be a detective. He had a limp after all, along with gray hair poking out the brim of the hat he wore. Then she considered that he might have been sent by the bald-headed man as retribution for the incident at the customer service counter earlier that week. Or maybe he was the man himself, wearing a disguise.

Get ahold of yourself. Remember you can do anything through Christ who strengthens you. Connie also realized that the ground beef she had bought would not last unless she got it into a refrigerator soon. Finally she turned around in the street and approached the apartment. To her relief, the man seemed to have disappeared. She thanked the Lord under her breath, parked the car, and began taking out the two plastic bags of groceries.

"Miss Ortiz."

The sound of a man's deep voice behind her made her jump. *Oh no, I'm being mugged! What should I do?* One of the bags slipped out of her hand, sending the head of lettuce rolling across the seat and onto the pavement.

"I'm sorry for startling you." His hand, clad in a black glove, slowly reached out to the road and picked up the head of lettuce.

Connie nearly cried out for help when she turned and found a craggy face peering into hers. He was only an older gentleman dressed in his trench coat. He gave her back the lettuce, torn and bruised by the encounter with the pavement.

"I'll buy you another head of lettuce," he said.

"No, no, that's all right." Her jittery hands managed to slip the lettuce back into the bag. No mugger would offer to buy her a head of lettuce. But he did know her name. Perhaps he was a detective after all. "Is there something you need?"

"Actually, yes."

Connie wondered what he could possibly want. Certainly she was no one of interest, only a humdrum store worker who had grabbed the attention of a handsome man for the first time in her life. Maybe the grocery store where she just bought the food had sent him to clarify the problem with money. But she'd cleared it up by taking away a banana, right?

"I–I don't understand what this is all about," Connie said. She walked gingerly to the door of her apartment and froze. It would be foolish to invite a stranger inside her apartment. What if he was someone of ill repute? But if she stood outside talking, the meat would go bad.

As if reading her mind he said, "If you have groceries to put in the refrigerator, I'll wait outside. I do need to talk to you, though. It's very important."

Connie nodded meekly. Inside she thought about the man in the trench coat waiting for her on the front doorstep and began imagining all sorts of possibilities. If this week hadn't been packed with excitement already, she was now ready to face her first inquisition by a genuine detective. She only prayed there wasn't a problem with her family. Not that her younger brothers could stay out of trouble—especially the youngest, Henry, or Enrique as Papa liked to call him. He'd already had a run-in with the law, having been caught selling marijuana.

When her parents found out about it, her mother cried and her father refused to speak to him. Papa ordered Henry out of the house. Connie tried to reach out to him with love as the Bible taught her to do. Henry refused to forgive their father for the way he had been treated. Now Connie feared perhaps Henry had delved into the drug scene again and that detectives, such as the one waiting for her outside the door, were on his trail.

She put away the groceries, went to get a glass of water, and then headed to the window to see the man still waiting for her on the doorstep. From the looks of him, he seemed ready to topple over. His fingers gripped the doorway. His legs wavered. She hastened outside where he had once more settled himself on the step. She wanted to invite him in but still felt uncertain about the whole encounter.

"I'm sure you're wondering why I'm here." The man slowly began to stand.

"Oh, please don't stand on my account. Yes," Connie said as she descended the step, then turned and faced him. "Has my brother done something wrong?"

"Your brother?" The man took off his hat, revealing sparse salt-and-pepper hair. Deep wrinkles decorated his face. The gray mustache he wore twitched back and forth.

"Yes, he was. . ." Connie could tell from the blank look on the man's face that this visit had nothing to do with her family. "Sorry. I thought you might be a detective. I'm not used to seeing a man standing in front of my apartment wearing a trench coat."

He chuckled and grasped the collar of his coat, straightening it in dignified fashion. He then took off his gloves and pocketed them. "I've been told by family that I should join the twenty-first century, but I refuse to part with my coat."

"I'm certain you've been called 'Sherlock' more than once."

The man lifted his head and laughed loudly. Connie glanced around to make certain no one down the street was listening. Yet she couldn't help smiling at his hearty laughter, putting her at ease for a moment.

"The reason I came to see you is because I noticed you at the yard sale last Saturday."

Connie stared, surprised by his comment. "Oh, really."

"Yes. And you bought a cuckoo clock from Mrs. Rowe, did you not?"

Her heart began to beat rapidly. What else did he know about her? He must really be a detective or maybe a private investigator.

He went on. "I would very much like to buy the clock from you. I will pay you handsomely for it."

Buy my cuckoo clock? His statement stunned her. Connie didn't know what to say. At first she wanted to tell the man he must be mistaking her for someone else, even though she knew it was a lie. She recalled the sale and how numerous people had begun arriving just as she decided to purchase the clock. In fact, it was the onslaught of customers all headed in the direction of the priceless item that made Connie decide to buy it outright. She didn't know at the time that someone else was actually interested in it.

The man began withdrawing his checkbook. "I would very much like the clock. I collect antiques, you see. And this is a very special clock."

His insistence unnerved her. She desperately wanted to tell him to go elsewhere and find his clock when the telltale sound of the cuckoo beckoned to her. It was the bird's chirp for the five o'clock hour. The cuckoo seemed to sing endlessly. The man paused with the checkbook in his hand, listening to the sound. Connie glanced back at her apartment and then at the man. Was that a tear she detected in the corner of his eye?

"As you can hear, I did buy the clock," Connie confirmed, "but it means a lot to me. My grandmother had one exactly like it."

"I'm sorry, but it means a great deal to me, too. That's why I'm prepared to offer you quite a bit for it." He took out a pen and clicked it open. "How does one thousand dollars sound?"

Connie stared in disbelief. One thousand dollars! Could this be real? In an instant she saw her money problems disappear quicker than water down a drain. She could buy a whole new wardrobe and matching shoes. Her clothing had been screaming for a lift, especially with her job at the department store. Even Donna had offered to buy her a few new blouses. She claimed the red top was getting a bit old with Connie wearing it twice a week.

"I can see you're seriously thinking about it," he said. "Shall I go ahead and write you out the check now?"

His quiet persuasiveness was deafening. It proved difficult to say no. But she had already become endeared to the quaint object that cheered her during the night, when all she had was the clock to keep her company. She didn't think it would happen so soon, but she loved the old clock and what it represented. The mere thought of parting with it, especially after the great deal she had found at the yard sale, made her pause. Yes, with the money he was about to give her, she could purchase an even better clock and maybe the list of clothing Donna had once drawn up for her. If she took his offer, there would be no clock on her wall to cheer her when she stepped through the door after a busy workday.

"I'm sorry, Mister. . ."

"Silas Westerfield." He extended his hand, which Connie shook.

"Mr. Westerfield, I'm sorry, but I've grown very partial to the clock. Like I said, it reminds me of the past—a miracle that happened, actually. I really can't part with it."

She watched the man's expectant expression fall. He put back the checkbook. "I see. So there's nothing I can do to change your mind? What if I upped the offer to twelve hundred?"

Connie shook her head, though her insides were screaming to say, *Yes!* "It means too much to me. I'm sorry."

"I see that we are very much alike, Miss Ortiz. If only you knew." He nodded his head and exhaled a long sigh. "I won't waste any more of your time." He bowed slightly and limped down the street to a taxi waiting for him on the corner. For an instant, Connie felt a wave of sadness followed by puzzlement at the man's final sentence to her. What did he mean that they were alike? Alike as in their desire to possess an old clock? Connie shook her head. If he was willing to spend twelve hundred dollars, he could certainly afford to buy another clock elsewhere. This was her possession after all; the clock God had given to her. She was convinced of it.

Yet the man's sorrowful face was not soon forgotten, nor was the exorbitant amount of money he'd offered to buy a dusty old clock from a yard sale. She began to consider it. Could it be that she had stumbled upon a unique treasure? Or did the clock hold something else of value that only the older man knew?

four

"You're crazy, girl! Absolutely crazy. Have you gone cuckoo like your clock?"

Connie was about to think she had as she made herself a rolled corn tortilla for dinner that night. She decided to call Donna about Silas Westerfield's offer, only to have her friend literally scream at her for not taking the man's generous offer. When she first told Donna about her visitor, her friend immediately asked if she had taken the money. When Connie answered no, Donna ranted and raved.

"And for your information, the particular cuckoo I'm referring to is you," Donna added. "Is that clock connected to you so much that you can't part with it even for twelve hundred dollars?"

Connie wanted to say yes. She was connected to it far greater emotionally than any item she had ever owned, save for the little princess glass shoe from her grandmother's collection. Perhaps no one would ever understand her feelings— except for God, who was there when it all happened. One had to be in the midst of it to see how a simple thing such as a clock could bring forth a response that money couldn't buy.

In her heart, Connie felt a peace with her purchase and with keeping it out of the hands of some stranger. Silas Westerfield was a well-to-do gentleman who could afford to buy another clock. He just happened to see her buy the clock at the yard sale and wanted it for himself. No doubt if Mrs.

Rowe knew how much he was willing to pay for it, she would have grabbed the clock out of Connie's hands and given it to him with a gold bow attached. Instead, Connie had snatched it up for seventy-five dollars, and now it was hers. She hoped the man would find another clock somewhere else, anywhere other than Connie's humble abode.

"I think you're making a big mistake," Donna admonished. "And I suppose you don't have any money now until payday."

"Don't worry, I'm not going to starve. God provides." *Sometimes through family*, she thought. In fact, she planned to ask her brother, Louis, for some money to tide her over until her paycheck arrived next week. A tortilla a day wouldn't be wise or healthy. Louis had always been protective of her when they were little, as they were the closest in age. He was making it big right now, repairing computers. But what would he say if she told him she needed the money because she had spent everything in her wallet on a silly clock instead of food? He would understand, she decided. After all, Louis was there at Grandma's when it all happened.

"I don't know about that religion of yours, Connie. Seems foolish to me sometimes."

"It's actually helped me in more ways than I can say, Donna. Talk to you soon."

They said good-bye, and Connie took the final bite of her tortilla while gazing at the clock. Right now it was silent with the cuckoo bird tucked inside its little dwelling before the half hour struck and the door flipped open for the little cuckoo to announce the time. She came over to admire it. For its age, the clock was in remarkable shape. It appeared as if Mrs. Rowe hadn't used it much, if ever, and had merely kept it in the attic for the longest time, just waiting for the right time to sell it.

Connie reached up to touch the smooth wood sides of the finely crafted instrument. God had divinely arranged this to be her clock of remembrance. God alone would have to bless Silas Westerfield with a clock, as He had blessed her. There was nothing else she could do.

Now she turned to her computer and e-mailed Louis, asking him if he would loan her fifty dollars. That should be enough to buy a few more groceries, pay the water bill, and leave her with money to fill the gas tank.

At that moment, the cuckoo bird appeared for its eight o'clock greeting. Connie listened, counting the eight cuckoos before the bird ducked inside. All at once she was a mere eight years old, gazing up in wonder at her grandmother's stately cuckoo clock hanging in the living room. When Mom told her they would be visiting Grandma, she was delighted. Family relations had been strained after her mother married "a foreigner," as Grandma put it.

Connie didn't consider her father foreign, even if he was born in Guatemala and much of his family still lived there. For a long time, Grandma and Mom were not on speaking terms. Finally Mom had decided the children needed to see their grandmother. She let go of the hurt caused by the separation, and they began visiting on a regular basis. Connie was eight at the time. Louis was seven, Henry six.

Upon arriving at Grandma's home for frequent visits, Connie immediately went to her favorite areas—like the back stairs where they liked to play hide-and-seek. Her favorite items were Grandma's princess shoe made of glass— which Connie often pretended to slip onto her tiny foot like Cinderella—a blue covered dish filled with fruited candies, and finally the cuckoo clock hanging on the living room wall.

Connie used to stand under the clock and wait patiently for the bird to emerge. When the bird did, she would gaze at it intently until the bird went into hiding and the door snapped shut.

One summer they decided on a lengthy visit when Papa was called away to take care of some business dealings with his family in Guatemala. They were to spend three weeks at Grandma's fascinating home. For a few days, she and her brothers roamed the large house, investigating the small rooms and the large walk-in pantry in the back, which was always cooler than the rest of the house. Inside the pantry was a long counter and enclosed shelves. Grandma always had bunches of bananas ripening on the counter and next to the bananas, large German coffee cakes sprinkled with cinnamon sugar she had made. She called it *kuchen,* and it was delicious.

Upstairs was a huge bathroom with an old-fashioned tub supported by clawed feet. Along the wall was a little trap door. Connie used to open the door and peer down the dark, foreboding shaft. When she heard it was a laundry chute that sent clothes to the washing machine in the basement, she would scramble down the metal staircase and to the washer where the chute door opened to reveal clothes gathered in a heap on the cold floor.

One day Henry dangled her dolly above the laundry chute, and with an evil grin, let it go.

"You killed my doll!" Connie screamed, looking into the chute to see her doll disappear into a deep, dark abyss. "Help! Help! Henry killed my doll."

Louis raced to find out what had happened, only to head to the basement and retrieve Connie's doll from the laundry piled up at the washing machine. After that incident, Connie made certain to hide her belongings from the mischievous Henry. He would not hesitate to drop other things down the chute if given the opportunity.

Besides the fascinating house, Grandma also liked to show off her garden. She had a green thumb, as some would put it. After Grandpa died, she continued planting and caring for the vegetable garden. Connie and her brothers went to investigate the vines of tomatoes and helped Grandma pull out a carrot or two. She admired how her grandma could do so many wonderful things, even though she lived all alone in her huge house with the awful laundry chute.

Then came the day Connie would never forget. It started normally, for the most part, except that Mom complained of a terrible headache that wouldn't go away. Suddenly Louis found her unconscious on the bathroom floor. Connie cried at the sight of her mother, unable to wake up even as she called out desperately to her. Grandma ran for the phone and dialed the rescue squad.

As they were lifting Mom's unconscious form onto a stretcher, the head EMT said she might have suffered a stroke. Connie didn't know what that was at the time, but she later learned that her mother had suffered a ruptured aneurysm in her brain. Most people died from such things.

God's hand had been upon her mother, even though Connie didn't realize it at the time. All she knew were the lonely days and nights while her mother was in the hospital in a deep sleep, as Grandma called it. A neighbor would come over and watch them while Grandma went to be with Mom. Connie never felt so alone in her life. Her pillow became wet with tears as she cried for her mother to come cuddle her. The only comfort she found during this difficult time was the cuckoo clock that she waited upon each hour. He was her friend, a cheerful interruption to the uncertainty happening around her.

Papa returned from Guatemala to be with Mom. He was the one who told them of the severity of Mom's condition. She stayed in a coma for two weeks. When she woke up without brain damage, everyone hailed it a miracle.

Connie walked over and touched the cuckoo clock she had purchased at the yard sale. She felt sorry for Silas Westerfield, having to decline his offer to buy the clock, but this instrument symbolized a miracle to her. Not only had her grandma's clock kept her company as a child during the most difficult time in her life, this clock reminded her of God's merciful hand in restoring her mother. She would never part with it, not for a million dollars. In her opinion, memories such as these were priceless.

She decided then to call her brother, Louis. Even though she had already e-mailed him, she wanted to talk about the clock and the emotions that had surfaced this night. She managed to catch him with his mouth full of food. Thinking of him before a gigantic smorgasbord reminded her of her sparse meal and her need for a little cash to make ends meet.

"So what are you eating?" she asked.

He went into a long exhortation about the necessity of eating foods that were good for you. He had been shopping at the health food store down the road and had made himself a vegetarian meal. "Do you realize how many preservatives are in all the food we eat?" he said before taking another noisy bite.

"I had a tortilla for dinner," Connie announced.

Louis laughed. "You still eat those things? I'll tell you if I even step into a Mexican restaurant, I get nauseated. That's all we ate growing up. Papa always had Mom make his favorite dishes, though at least she did manage to talk him out of having his main meal at noon like he was used to doing in Guatemala. And remember the time she forced him to eat her German food of sauerbraten and red cabbage? He turned as purple as the cabbage, if I recall."

Connie had to laugh, thankful Louis was also in the mood to take a stroll down memory lane. She glanced at her clock and told him about her purchase, along with the memories that resurfaced, such as Grandma's house and the time their mother took ill.

"I don't remember much about it," Louis confessed. "I was only seven. I remember the loud noise the rescue squad made when it came to the house. I remember that Mom wouldn't wake up. In fact, she didn't wake up for the longest time, did she?"

"It seemed like a long time, but actually it was only two weeks. I know of others who have suffered brain injuries where it takes much longer. I just heard the other day of a man who woke up after nineteen years. Can you imagine? And his wife was still there at his bedside, waiting for him. When he had been in the car accident that put him in a coma, they were newly married."

Louis sighed over the phone. "Glad those days with Mom are long past. And I'm glad we didn't have to go through anything like nineteen years. So what do you need, Connie? I know this can't be a social call. Money?"

Connie gaped at his presumption. Was she that easy to read? She had asked Louis for money before, but the times were few and far between. "I did catch myself a little short this month after using my spending money to buy the clock. Could you spare fifty? I e-mailed you about it, but a phone call is a little more personal."

"Fifty, eh? Okay, I'll transfer some money to your account. And this time you don't need to pay me back."

"What? Of course I do."

"No. Call it an early birthday gift."

"But my birthday isn't for three months."

"No problem. You're my sis. I'm sure I owe you for some kind of payback at one time or another in our lives."

"The only incident that comes to mind is the time you decided to float my play dishes down the creek. Remember that? I screamed at you and told you to go get them. You just stood there on the bank, watching them bob up and down, saying what cool boats they made. For all you know, I could have permanent psychological damage for not having play dishes growing up. Maybe that's why I can't make myself decent meals. I've been deprived."

Louis laughed at her joke. "Okay, then this is payback time for losing your play dishes. You can buy a new set."

Connie giggled, thinking of a set she wouldn't mind owning—the tiny china dishes decorated in rose print, enclosed in a wee picnic basket. She had seen it in a country store once. After hanging up the phone a few moments later, she felt better. Louis never failed to cheer her with his positive outlook on life. He had been successful at whatever he put his mind to, including school, college, and now his computer business. Mom and Papa were proud of him.

Now if only she had a better relationship with her other brother, Henry. He tended to be a loner. He and Louis didn't get along at all, especially after his run-ins with the law.

Connie did what she could to reach out to him, but Henry was his own person and did what he pleased in life. At least she was grateful to have the open communication with Louis. She wasn't too proud to ask him for a loan now and then. And he always obliged.

Connie then thought about Silas Westerfield's offer of twelve hundred dollars that would have taken her out of this monetary slump and then some. The mere notion he wanted to give her such an exorbitant sum for a clock from a yard sale left her puzzled. Why did he want it so much? Did he know something intriguing about the clock that she didn't? He must if he was a collector of antiques. Perhaps she had stumbled upon something huge when she bought the clock and didn't even realize it.

Connie ventured over to study the timepiece. There was nothing unusual about it from what she could tell. It was in perfect working order. She didn't think it could be as valuable as he said, but it must be. She had heard stories of people who had stumbled upon great treasures in attics, basements, and at yard sales. She used to watch that program on television where people would take their most treasured items and have them appraised for their value. Maybe she should take this clock to such a place and find out its true worth.

Connie shook her head. It didn't matter. Silas Westerfield seemed compliant with her request to keep the clock, and she had a treasured memory that cost but seventy-five dollars. She would be content with that, at least for now.

⁂

Connie arrived for work the next morning, tired from the nightmare that besieged her during the night. In it, Silas Westerfield showed up at her doorstep at 2:00 a.m., ordering her to give him back the clock. She could still see his gnarled face and gray eyes blazing as he waved the checkbook at her. *If you don't give me that clock, I'll make your life miserable, like sending you a dozen angry customers to mob your service desk!* From beneath the folds of his huge trench coat came a parade of angry customers, all waving merchandise and demanding that Mr. Drexer fire her and toss her into the street to become a helpless beggar.

"Hello out there!" hailed a friendly voice.

Connie whirled and caught her elbow on the corner of the desk. Pain shot through her arm. "Ouch!"

"Are you okay?" The calm face and dark brown eyes of Lance Adams stared into hers.

"Y—yeah. Just got up on the wrong side of the bed, I think." She nearly told him about the escapade at the grocery store, the corn tortilla for dinner, and the man with the trench coat who wanted her precious clock. Likely after all the stories, he would recommend commitment to some insane asylum. Instead she fumbled in the drawer for slips of papers and pens to start the day.

"You look like something's bothering you."

"I didn't sleep very well last night." Besides the dream, her stomach kept her up with cries for nourishment. The corn tortilla for dinner hadn't lasted long. Finally, in the middle of the night, Connie made herself a lettuce salad to tide her over until breakfast. She planned to make another trip to the grocery store after work for more substantial food purchases. Before she left that morning, she checked her banking account online and found that Louis had transferred the fifty dollars. She thanked God for the generosity of her brother. Now she could buy good stuff, like some delectable apple crumb muffins.

"So did you decide to sell him the clock?" Donna asked, bopping up behind the desk.

Connie cringed, wishing Donna hadn't brought up the subject of the clock in front of Lance. "No. I told you I wouldn't sell it for a million dollars." Connie tried to look busy in the hopes this would blow over.

"Mr. Adams, did you hear what happened?" Donna now inquired of Lance. When he shook his head, Donna launched right into the tale without giving a thought as to how Connie might feel. "And this elderly man comes to her door, asking to buy the clock for twelve hundred dollars. Can you imagine? Twelve hundred for a clock that only cost—how much did you pay for it at the yard sale, Connie?"

Connie pretended not to hear her until Donna stepped up and nearly shouted the question in her ear.

"Seventy-five," she said in a low voice.

Lance raised his eyebrow. "Really. He must want it very badly."

"I'll say. And knowing how poor Connie is, I would have jumped at the chance. I mean, she complains she doesn't have money to fill her gas tank, then this man pops up at her front doorstep offering her cold hard cash. I don't understand why she wouldn't take it."

Connie felt her face begin to heat up. Now Lance knew her financial situation along with the clock episode. If only she could put a cork in Donna's mouth. But when would that ever stop her? She rattled on about it for another five minutes and even turned to several of the cashiers who had come up, telling them the tale of the man in the trench coat who wanted Connie's clock for "twelve hundred smackeroos."

"This must be some clock," Sally said, staring at Connie

with a look that made her all the more uncomfortable. "Can I come see it after work, Connie?"

"It's just a cuckoo clock."

"Does it really work?"

"Of course."

A crowd of employees now gathered around the customer service counter, giving their opinions as to whether they would have accepted a twelve-hundred-dollar check for a clock that cost seventy-five. The majority agreed they would have jumped at the chance. Only a few believed that a high-priced antique was worth holding on to. The battle intrigued Connie. At first she wanted to sweep the encounter under the rug, but the employees' enthusiasm proved infectious. "I guess it must be a unique clock," she agreed. "Maybe I should give tours." *That would be one way to get myself out of a financial pinch. Charge a five-dollar admission fee for a glimpse of the mysterious cuckoo clock.*

"Great!" Sally exclaimed. "When can we have a tour?"

"Yes, yes!" other clamored. "When will you let us come see it?"

Connie observed the assortment of eager faces, each one wishing to see her famous clock. Maybe she shouldn't let the opportunity slip her by. How often she thought about reaching out to coworkers with the saving message of the gospel, but could never quite find a way to do it. Now she had the opportunity of showing them the clock God had provided and sharing the miracle of her mother's recovery from an aneurysm. Perhaps God might use the clock to bring people closer to Him.

"Let's have a luncheon on Saturday," she decided. "I'm off that day. And those of you who aren't off, maybe you can stop by on your break and join us."

Everyone pounced on the idea of a get-together. They all talked at once about having lunch and seeing the infamous clock. Connie tore off a sheet of yellow paper from a legal pad and had people sign up to bring a dish to share. She bubbled over with excitement at the thought of this luncheon turning into an outreach of sorts. When the others had left to perform their duties, Lance stepped up.

"Guess you do know how to gather a crowd," he observed. "And it just so happens, I have Saturday off."

Connie glanced at him while trying to contain the glee welling up within her. Not only was there the opportunity of an outreach to the other employees, but Lance Adams planned on gracing the event as well. "Great! How about signing up to bring something?"

"I don't cook, so how does a bottle of soda sound?"

Connie giggled and scribbled down his name along with the item he volunteered to bring. "Maybe you can make it two bottles. Or a bottle of soda and a gallon of spring water." She tapped a pen on the counter in thought. "I'll need paper plates and cups. Disposable forks. Napkins."

"If you need me to bring anything else, just let me know. I know you're short on cash."

The joy of the event quickly soured at his knowledge of her tight finances. "I'm fine," she said swiftly. "God provides."

"I agree He does, and sometimes He provides through the giving of others. So if you need anything, please call. And if you don't, I'll get mighty upset."

Lance wandered off toward the management offices, leaving Connie with her yellow sheet of paper and warmth that invaded her heart. *Dear God, I'm so glad You brought the cuckoo clock into my life! Look at the blessing it's bringing. Now every-one is coming over for a lunch—including the star of the show, Lance Adams.* If this was any indication of what might lay ahead, Connie decided the clock was the best investment she'd ever made.

five

Connie bustled around her apartment, readying everything for the luncheon at noon that would bring several friends from work along with her special guest, Lance Adams. She smoothed the rumpled fabric of the old sofa that once stood in Grandma's living room, straightened out the magazine rack, and took up a feather duster to give Mr. Cuckoo a shine. So far the bird had been doing his thing all morning and right on schedule, much to her delight. The piece appeared proud and majestic, hanging on the wall of the living room, ready for the array of curious onlookers.

She wondered what Lance would think of her home. As an executive, he must live in a fine place with new furniture and high-tech equipment. Actually, she knew very little about him, even if he did know everything about her—courtesy of Donna. The idea made her feel miffed. At times she wished Donna would stay out of her life but knew that attitude wouldn't be in keeping with her Christianity. Somehow Connie envisioned the opportunity of reaching Donna with the gospel message. Instead, she found her friend's ways grating on her nerves. Maybe God was using Donna to do a little refining in her own heart—to have patience and seek peace no matter what circumstances might come her way.

Connie set to work making up one of her grandmother's recipes on her father's side, a dish of stuffed tortillas with black beans for lunch. She only recalled meeting her foreign relatives twice in her life. Both times they came to the house for Christmas when Connie was young. Her *abuelita*, as her paternal grandmother was known, couldn't speak a word of English. Connie found herself unable to communicate at all except for a few words of Spanish she picked up from her father. Papa's two brothers who also came spoke broken English, and her *abuelito*, or grandfather, said nothing but merely stared into space. Somehow Connie never felt much of a connection to her father's side of the family. Perhaps she ought to consider changing that somehow, maybe even by joining one of those mission trips to Guatemala. That would be a good way to see her relatives.

Now Connie considered the luncheon and what she would say about the clock. She didn't want to preach, but she did want them to know the miracles God had worked in her family. She hoped her hospitality skills would help make Lance feel welcome. Thankfully with Louis's money she was able to purchase items for the luncheon like matching paper plates, cups, and napkins.

Perhaps it was in her blood to throw a nice gathering for others. Papa loved to throw gatherings for people from his workplace. Often he had associates come to their home where he cooked up food native to Guatemala. The house would be filled with the scent of corn, cilantro, and onions. The guests would all laugh and share stories, to the wide eyes of her and her brothers who only stared at the assortment of people gathered around the table. Sometimes the guests would give them presents. Connie still had the small furry monkey a guest had given to her during one of Papa's dinners. She wondered if Lance might bring her a present. *You're crazy, girl. Just crazy.* Lance appeared the dignified type, not the fuzzy kind that would give a lady stuffed animals and boxes of chocolates.

The doorbell rang. Connie looked up at the clock to find there was still fifteen minutes to go before the guests were scheduled to arrive. Who could be here so early? She checked between the blinds to find Lance standing there. She might have guessed it would be him. It seemed his character, though most men were usually late, as her brothers often were. Many times her mother yelled at Louis and Henry to hurry up. She opened the door to find Lance holding a gift bag.

"I figured I would come a little early and see if you needed help setting up."

What a gentleman, she thought in admiration. He then presented her with the bag. "Just a little something."

Connie turned to one side, trying to conceal her flushing face from his gaze. She took the bag and opened it to find a small stuffed bird.

"The tag says it's a cuckoo bird. He's called Clarence."

"Clarence the cuckoo," she said with a laugh. So Lance was indeed the stuffed animal, chocolate bonbon type after all. "Thank you very much." She proudly displayed Clarence on the antique table in the foyer.

"Looks like you have everything ready." He nodded, staring at the matching cups, plates, and napkins along with a small centerpiece of flowers. "Is there anything I need to do?"

Connie shook her head. "Just make yourself at home."

"Oops, forgot the drinks in the car. Be right back." He made a mad dash to his vehicle parked out front. Connie peeked out the window to see that he drove a navy blue compact car that sparkled in the rays of sunlight. She could tell from the looks of the car that he liked things to be clean and neat. She was grateful she had spent extra time earlier that morning dusting and straightening her humble abode. She didn't want him thinking she was messy, especially after what happened at the customer service counter the first day they met. The vision of the candy wrappers and spilled soda on the floor still made her cringe.

Lance returned with a bottle of soda and a container of spring water. He followed her into the kitchen where she placed the drinks inside the fridge to chill. "You eat sparse," he noted, scanning the empty shelves.

Connie had forgotten about her meager food supply. The shelves were bare but for the few items she had purchased the other day. He looked at her as if remembering Donna's discussion of her financial situation. *He probably thinks I go to the neighborhood soup kitchen for my meals.* "I don't eat very much."

"Maybe we should think about a cost of living raise at the store," he said as though thinking out loud. "I'll have to check into it."

If only Donna hadn't said anything about my money troubles. But a raise would be nice, she had to admit. Keeping up with the rent, plus utilities, car bill, and food did take every penny out of her check. She refused to say anything one way or the other but allowed him to mull over the idea.

Just then the doorbell rang. The other employees from the store had arrived, carrying delectable luncheon entrees while chattering away. It didn't take long for the small apartment to feel crowded, yet Connie was glad for the companionship. How often she had envisioned coordinating a get-together for the employees but never quite knew how to go about it. Now thanks to a fortunate purchase at a yard sale, everything had come together. She directed them to the kitchen where they set down their food items on the counter.

All at once Mr. Cuckoo came forth for his noontime sere-nade. Her coworkers rushed to the living room to watch the bird perform. The noise continued for some time until the bird suddenly disappeared behind the tiny trap door.

"How sweet!" Sally exclaimed in glee. "I absolutely love it! I can see now why you want to hold on to it, Connie. What a wonderful find."

"Yes, but you can get that model of clock anywhere," Donna interjected. "I looked it up on the Internet myself. In fact it only sells for a few hundred dollars at most, depending on what it does and how often you need to wind it. It's not as elaborate as some of them, which can cost over a thousand. So I say if someone wants this clock that badly and for twelve hundred dollars, let him have it. For two hundred bucks you can get a clock almost exactly like it and pocket the rest of the cash."

Anger began stirring within Connie, and the guests had only been there ten minutes. She ushered them to the small dining area, hoping to avoid a major confrontation between her and Donna. She didn't want to debate money or anything else. She knew if she said anything, the emotion it raised might squelch whatever God wanted to do among her guests. She showed them the food and encouraged them to help themselves. Everyone obliged, taking paper plates and dishing up the food. Several mentioned how delicious Connie's tor-tillas were, including Lance.

"This is great," he told her, "but I thought you didn't like Mexican food."

"This is a special recipe from Guatemala, not Mexico. And I do eat Spanish food. The same as I'm sure you eat roast beef, even though you've probably had it every Sunday while you were growing up."

Lance looked at her in surprise. "How did you know that?"

"You seem like a person raised on meat and potatoes."

"Yep, an all-American guy," he added with a wink.

To Connie's disappointment, he took a seat at the other end of the table and began engaging Sally in conversation. She had hoped he might want to sit with her after the encouraging meetings the past few days. Instead, Donna sat beside her and again voiced her opinion about the clock and the way Connie had mismanaged the wealthy gentleman who came calling. Her teeth began to grind in agitation. Tension filled her muscles. If only there was some polite way to tell Donna to lay off the whole scene with Silas Westerfield. Finally Connie managed to change the subject by sharing with others why she kept the clock. The table grew silent as they heard of Connie's mother and how a cuckoo clock had kept her company at her grandmother's home while her mother lay in a coma at the hospital.

"That's awful," Sally said in sympathy. "I can see now why money can't replace something like that."

"But it isn't the same clock as your grandma's," Donna pointed out. "You could get any other cuckoo clock, and it would still serve the same purpose."

"Perhaps, but this clock looks very similar to my grandmother's," Connie answered in defense. "And I know all about those clocks you're mentioning. They're half the size of this one and with all kinds of newfangled modifications. This is an older version, and one I will treasure. So can we just let it go?"

Donna sat back in her seat with a stunned expression on her face. Connie began clearing the plates and brought out the dessert. Looking around the table at the assortment of thoughtful faces, she hoped the exchange between her and Donna hadn't chilled the meeting.

Suddenly she noticed Lance missing from the group. She peeked around the corner and found him in the living room, staring at the clock in obvious fascination. When she called him to come have dessert, he whirled and returned to the table without saying a word. The rest of her guests began discussing sports, movies they had seen, and other items of interest in their lives. After some time passed, several of them bid Connie farewell as they needed to return to work. Donna and Sally hung out awhile longer, talking about the yard sales they had been to and some of the bargains they had discovered. When they were ready to leave for the spring sales at the mall, Donna looked back at Connie as if ready to give her another opinion. She then tossed her head, thanked her for arranging the lunch, and took off with Sally. Connie tried hard not to take offense by what had happened, but sometimes she wondered if it was wise having Donna as a friend.

Connie returned to the living room and again found Lance staring at her clock. He stood in a thoughtful pose with his hands tucked into the pockets of his trousers, gazing up at it as she often had. He seemed mesmerized by the piece. Maybe like her, he had seen a similar clock in his youth. Or perhaps the memories she shared about her mother had affected him in some way. She wanted to ask him about it, when suddenly he reached up and began taking the instrument off the wall hanger.

At once Connie came forward. "Is something wrong?"

He jerked around, his hands trembling, nearly losing his grip on the piece. Connie gasped, praying he wouldn't drop it.

"No, no. I was just looking is all." He slowly returned the clock to its proper resting place. "Where did you say you got it?"

"A neighbor down the street from me. Claudia Rowe."

"Claudia Rowe," he repeated, still gazing at the clock. "And she sold it to you for seventy-five dollars?"

"Yes."

"It's in excellent condition. Where did she keep it?"

"A box in the attic or so she told me. I don't think she ever had it out—or at least not for very long. I saw no scratches on it, wear and tear, or anything. Except for the dust, it looked practically brand-new."

"Sad she never had it displayed."

Connie looked at him, puzzled. "Why? That means I got a great deal on a clock in mint condition. She wanted to get rid of it anyway. She's moving. I guess she had too much clutter."

"So that's why she had the sale?"

Connie nodded. "She already sold the house. More than likely she will leave by the time summer rolls around. I hope she has another yard sale, though. I would love to see if she has anything else stored up there in the attic."

Lance said nothing but only continued to stare at the clock. "So you wouldn't consider parting with it, would you?"

"Huh? Don't tell me you want it, too?"

"Not for me, but I was thinking if that man wanted it—"

"As I said earlier, the clock means a lot to me."

"Yes, but maybe it means a lot to others as well. And certainly you could use the money, right?"

Connie gaped before turning away. It seemed Donna had hoodwinked Lance into trying to make her give up the clock for a fat check. This was becoming more aggravating by the minute. "I really think this is my problem. I know you may be the manager-in-training, but that doesn't mean I can't make my own decisions."

"I just want you to consider all the angles here. I can tell the clock means a great deal to you because of the past. But like Donna said, there are other clocks in this world."

"Yes, and there are other clocks for antique hunters as well. And despite what Donna said, I don't need the money that badly. The memory of how God saved my mother is more important to me than whether I have filet mignon for dinner." She turned away and marched back to the kitchen. Why was everyone fighting with her over this clock? Didn't any of her words at the table matter to them? Here she had tried to use the clock as a means of sharing God's blessing, and now everyone wanted to talk her out of keeping it. Could they be so callous as to think that money means more than memories?

Her aggravation soon turned into anger. She shook her head when Lance offered help with the cleanup. He was in the same category as Donna as far as she was concerned. Maybe it would be better for him to make a move on Donna instead. They both operated on the same wavelength when it came to getting ahead in the world.

Lance remained in the kitchen, even after she'd refused his help. "Connie, I don't want you angry over this. I only think you need to consider other points of view besides your own. That's why the Bible says there's wisdom in a multitude of counselors."

Connie snorted at the thought of either Donna or him as counselors. Right now they were both bothersome gnats flying around in her face. "There are millions of clocks in the world. Let Mr. Westerfield and others find some at yard sales."

"That's what I'm trying to say, Connie. There are millions of clocks for you to choose from, also. Maybe you should let the man have it, and you find something else when the time and money is right."

She must've had a horrible look on her face, for he quickly backpedaled, offered a hasty good-bye, and headed for the door.

Connie inhaled a deep breath to calm herself. Why was this happening to her? After cleaning up, she plopped down on the sofa to stare at the clock. Why, out of all the clocks in this world, did this one have to mean so much to Silas Westerfield? And now even strangers were going to bat for him. She tried to consider this from the older man's viewpoint but couldn't. The man was obviously a dealer who found something at a yard sale that caught his eye, and she had snatched it away. Wasn't there a saying for such things? Finders keepers, losers weepers?

She sat mulling over it all—Silas Westerfield, Donna, and finally Lance. She was certain Lance entered his opinion out of a concern for her financial status. He had seen the empty fridge. He thought it would do her wallet good to sell the clock and look for another. He wanted what was best for her. Perhaps the conversation showed that Lance truly cared about her.

Connie gazed at her purchase. Little did he realize, but what was best for her right now was this clock. It brought her companionship and a wealth of fond memories from days gone by. If only she didn't feel so troubled. Instead of joy, she now wrestled with confusion. *God*, she prayed, *help me sort this all out, somehow, someway.*

six

Over the next few weeks, little was said at work about the clock. It was as if the cuckoo had been a passing fancy and now everyone's attention turned to their daily lives. Connie was glad things had quieted down. The clock still remained the focal point in Connie's apartment, especially on her days off when Mr. Cuckoo faithfully announced the time every half hour. The rhythmic ticking assisted her when mopping the floor or even cleaning out a corner cupboard where she had put away old cards received over the years. Searching through them one day, she found a couple from her grandmother, etched out in her stately writing. These cards were worth their weight in gold.

To her surprise, tucked away inside one card she found the recipe for kuchen, the famous German coffee cake that Grandma always made when they came visiting. She gasped when she saw it, having forgotten that Grandma sent her the recipe in the hope that the tradition would be carried on within the family. Scanning it, Connie decided to splurge a bit with the paycheck she had recently received and buy the ingredients to make a few cakes. No doubt the employees would love the baked treats when they came into work the next morning. She could just imagine the exclamations as they cut healthy wedges of the coffee cake to accompany the morning coffee, brewed strong the way Donna always made it.

Connie began assembling the ingredients after a quick trip

to the grocery store. While waiting for the milk to scald in the saucepan, she reflected on the luncheon at her home and Lance as he walked about examining everything, especially the cuckoo clock. For days afterward, she analyzed the comments he had made. At church last Sunday he appeared rather aloof, offering her a pleasant good morning but otherwise ignoring her. At work she hoped for a few clues as to why he was so emphatic that she accept the older man's offer. He said nothing about it. It didn't matter anyway. By now, Mr. Westerfield likely had located a different antique clock to satisfy his need. Still she wished she knew the motivation behind Lance's insistence. If he did care about her, as she hoped, then she prayed he would understand her need to keep the clock.

Bubbles began appearing on the milk's surface when Connie removed the pan to a trivet to let it cool. What a pleasant way to spend the day—in the kitchen with her hands immersed in fragrant dough, working to make her grandmother's beloved recipe, with the cuckoo chiming in the background. There was nothing better except perhaps an outing with Lance, if he ever offered one. At one time he did suggest they go out for gourmet pizza. Connie figured he'd forgotten about the invitation. Either that, or he'd found someone better to dine with than a woman who loved memories more than money. She began adding ingredients to the warm milk in the bowl until a soft dough formed. The pleasant aroma of yeast was more soothing than a cup of hot tea.

Before long the dough had risen beautifully, with the help of a trick she learned from a cooking show—placing the mixture in a warm oven with a small pan of water on a separate rack. Parceling out the dough into four pans and drizzling each with butter, cinnamon, and sugar, she placed the pans back into the warm oven to rise one last time.

Grandma would be proud of her if she were alive. She would laugh and talk about her days as a young girl when she lived on the farm. Connie wished she were still alive. How she would love to share about what was happening in her life right now—and especially after buying the clock. *At least there's a little of you here, Grandma, even if you aren't alive to see it.* When Connie removed the crusty brown treats some time later, she stared at her creations in approval before snapping pictures on the camera. *Just wait until I tell my brother Louis that I made kuchen,* she thought proudly.

At work the next day, Connie juggled the bread, along with her purse, while struggling to open the door that led to the employee lounge. Suddenly a familiar face peered into hers as his hand reached out to open the door.

"What's that?" he inquired.

Connie looked up into the face of Lance Adams who helped her with the breads she had brought, carrying two of them to the table.

"It's something I made," Connie said breathlessly, placing the baked goods near the coffee and cups. Several employees gathered around to stare at the treats like puppies with their tongues hanging out.

"Coffee cake!" Sally exclaimed.

"No, it's kuchen," Connie corrected. "I made it."

"Wow." Everyone looked at her in appreciation. Connie brought out a knife from inside her purse and cut the bread into wedges, then served them on paper napkins.

"This is fantastic," Sally said. "Can you get me the recipe?"

"It takes a long time to make," Connie confessed. "It's like a yeast bread."

"So you can't make it in a bread machine?"

"Oh, no. You have to make this the old-fashioned way, like my grandma used to do. It's a German coffee cake."

Lance had already eaten one piece and was cutting himself a second. "This is really great, Connie," he said in appreciation. "You're a woman of many talents."

"Well, not really."

"Of course you are." He acknowledged the swarm of employees that descended on the lounge when word spread of homebaked treats waiting for them. "You know how to bring everyone together. You have a gift for hospitality, which is really needed nowadays. Everyone seems so busy all the time. They tend to forget the number two rule of loving your neighbor. But you certainly haven't."

Connie was glad to see Lance talking to her again. She figured he was still upset over the way she'd spoken to him at the luncheon. Instead, he made a few more encouraging remarks, including how great the bread tasted and if he could also have the recipe to send to his mother back home. "She likes to make fancy breads," he added.

"Sure. I'd be glad to write it out." *Guess you scored big-time with Lance, Connie ol' girl, even if the conversation at the luncheon didn't go so well.* She enjoyed the warm fuzzy feeling floating around inside her. With the clock but a distant memory, perhaps everything would get back on track in their newfound relationship. The outlook improved all the more when Lance asked her to go over some ideas with him before the store opened for business that morning.

She followed him to his office, thinking how nice he looked for his job. He was impeccably dressed in fancy pressed trousers and a navy blue shirt. The navy blue solid-colored tie he wore matched the shirt to a tee. Connie loved seeing a man dressed in solid colors and often bought Louis shirts with matching ties for Christmas.

"Come on in."

Connie entered the small office to find a rubber plant decorating a corner and a desk filled with mementos. Several pictures graced the windowsill including, to Connie's dismay, several portraits of women.

"Have a seat," he offered. "I just wanted to tell you first off that I appreciate the many ways you've been bringing the employees together."

Connie sat back in her seat, surprised by this statement.

"I wasn't kidding when I said you have a gift for hospitality. As it is, I've been trying to think of ways to have the employees interact. I'd like to have us more like family, working together to run this store. And I'd like you to think about heading up a hospitality committee."

"A hospitality committee?"

"You know, come up with ways to bring the employees together. I know in other companies there are business softball leagues, company picnics, that sort of thing. Would you be interested in heading up such a committee?"

His dark brown eyes leveled directly on hers. Her heart skipped a beat. "I guess so, if I can find people to help me with it. I'm sure Donna would jump at it."

"That's a good idea. I don't expect you to do this all on your own. We need each other to make things work."

Connie began fiddling with her watch, sliding it around on her wrist. "Sure, okay."

Lance smiled. "Good. I knew I could rely on you, Connie. So. . ." He began pushing papers around on his desk. "How's that infamous clock of yours?"

Connie stared, unable to believe he had brought up the subject out of thin air. If he was going to ask her again to sell the clock to the elderly man, she might tell him to find someone else to run the hospitality committee. "It's working fine, if that's what you mean."

"You still don't plan to part with it?"

"No, I don't. I'm sure the man has already found another clock." Uneasiness swept over her. Yes, she would do just about anything else for Lance Adams, like helping with his committee, but she would not sell her clock. "By the way, I do have something I want to discuss."

He perked up as if he couldn't wait to hear it. When she launched into questions about the new policy of drawing up money orders at the customer service counter, he frowned. Surely he didn't mean to discuss the clock more? She tried hard not to read into his nonverbal reaction, but couldn't help the confusion that began to build. How she wished she could make him understand where she was coming from. Like the kuchen recipe and the princess glass slipper, the clock was a part of her past and would remain in the present to bring joy to her and others. Maybe if she could convince him that it was her witnessing tool of sorts, a reminder of God's miracle in preserving her mother's life, maybe then he wouldn't worry about the elderly antique dealer or her monetary situation.

The meeting promptly ended without another mention of the clock, to Connie's relief. But she couldn't help noticing that Lance's gaze followed her out the door, and with it, an obvious disappointment over the decision she had made. Well, it was not his choice. It was hers and God's. And right now she felt completely comfortable with it.

☙

Connie left work that day with mixed feelings. While she liked Lance and thought him handsome to boot, his preoccupation with her cuckoo clock irritated her to no end. *I guess he assumed I would take his advice since he's the assistant manager,* she thought, pulling into a gas station. The action of filling the tank and paying the cashier reminded her of everyone's solution to her financial situation—selling the clock. Thankfully, at this point she was doing fine. After careful budgeting and the money from Louis, she was in the clear for the rest of the month and then some. She even had a bit left over, perhaps to do a bit more browsing at some yard sales this coming weekend. She still needed to locate that rocking chair for Sally who mentioned it to her on lunch break earlier that day.

Connie continued on until she spied an older man limping along the sidewalk, trying to manage two sacks of heavy groceries. In an instant, she pulled over to the side. Normally she would never consider picking up a stray person off the street, but the man appeared harmless and in need. "Do you need a ride?"

"I was going to wait for the Connector there at the corner," he said, mentioning the transit service in town.

"Where do you live? Maybe I can take you there."

He paused as if to consider the offer, then said, "Blue Ridge Avenue."

"That's not far from where I live." Connie opened the trunk, came around, and loaded the two sacks. Seeing the multitude of heavy cans in one of the bags, she wondered how the man managed such a load this far from the store.

"You're very kind," he added, gingerly settling into the front seat. "I believe we've met before."

Connie blinked. She didn't think she had ever seen him until she recalled the man in the trench coat waiting for her at the door. He did appear familiar with his characteristic limp, though this man wore a cardigan sweater. "Have we?" She took off down the street.

"Yes, we have met," he concurred. "Several weeks ago. I offered you money for a cuckoo clock."

At this Connie felt the red flush entering her cheeks. *Oh no! Why out of all the elderly men in the world did I have to pick up him?* "Oh, really?" she managed to say.

"Of course you must remember that. I was waiting by your front doorstep. I suppose it was a little bit presumptuous of me to be waiting there, expecting you to hand your clock over to some stranger."

Connie said nothing, though inwardly she agreed with him.

"Although I must say I'm particularly fond of antiques. And that clock has sentimental value. Worth the cost and more."

"I know."

He looked over at her, puzzled.

"It means a great deal to me, too. My grandmother owned a clock exactly like it."

"I see."

"And I stayed with her during a particularly hard time in my life. I was only a little girl, and to have your mother near death in the hospital, it brings about feelings that are very hard to describe. Feelings of loneliness, of emptiness, wondering if anyone will love you and take care of you."

"So you stayed with your grandmother while your mother was ill?"

Connie nodded, surprised by the tears that erupted in her eyes. She flicked them away to concentrate on the road before her. "Yes. The clock helped keep my mind off my mother. She did get better, which I was thankful for. I felt that God had given me the clock to remind me of the time He'd blessed my family."

"I see," the man said again. "So there's no possible way you would reconsider. Even if I offered you more than I offered before?"

Connie noticed the determined look he wore on his face. Even after sharing her innermost secret, the man was not swayed. Why was the clock worth that much in his eyes?

"I'm sorry, but I have no interest in selling. I hope you understand." She drove up Blue Ridge Street. "Which house is it?"

"The brick one, just up there." When the car stopped in front, the man thanked her and began removing his wallet.

"You don't need to pay me for the ride."

"Well then, thank you. You've been very kind."

Connie went to retrieve the groceries. "I'm sorry about the clock, but I had hoped you might find another one."

"I wish I could," he said sadly, taking the bags from her. "But there's only one like it in the world. Good day."

Connie watched the man walk gingerly to his home, pondering his words. What did he mean there was only one like it in the world? Could the clock really be that valuable? Now she couldn't wait to go home and look at it. Maybe she had actually stumbled upon something of tremendous worth and didn't even know it. Only an antique dealer, with an eye for such things, would know the value of the clock. The mere idea it might be worth thousands intrigued her.

She came home in time to see the cuckoo bird emerge for the five o'clock round of chirping. She took the clock off the wall and examined it. What untold mysteries surrounded this timepiece? It wasn't like that clay box a curator once found that supposedly held the bones of Jesus' brother in it. But there must be something of intrinsic value to have the man pursue it, enough for him to claim there's only one like it in the world. To Connie's eyes it was only an old cuckoo with a pleasing sound that rekindled childhood memories. But he spoke of it as an object of great worth.

Connie held the clock tight in her arms. "If that's true, Mr. Cuckoo, then I would be a fool to let you go."

seven

Connie awoke the next morning feeling worse than she had in weeks. A tension headache teased her, along with a sour feeling that stemmed from her circumstances. Ever since the meeting with Silas Westerfield, she sensed the peace of God leave her. She couldn't imagine why. Many times over the course of her life she felt God's displeasure with her decisions, and last night was the latest example. She still believed her intentions were good as far as the clock was concerned, but the older man's unmistakable sadness, along with his strange comments, raised a three-pronged battle of wills within her. One side questioned the idea of selling a clock that meant everything to her, simply to fulfill the desire of some antique dealer. It parleyed with the side that felt she should be willing to let go of the clock if God desired it. Yet another wondered whether the clock did have more of an intrinsic value than she was led to believe. After all, Silas Westerfield did say there was only one like it in the world. The whole situation left her feeling anxious and upset. At work she found herself snapping at the customers, especially at a lady who couldn't find her sales receipt.

"I'm sure I had it. I might have dropped it outside the door while trying to get my baby into the car seat."

Connie nearly growled. "I'm sorry, but we can only give refunds with a dated sales receipt." Her fingers felt for the pain throbbing at her temples.

"Can you make an exception just this once?"

No one makes exceptions for me, she thought. "I can give you a direct exchange if you don't have a receipt." The pain in her head mounted with each passing moment.

"But I can't use this toy. It's too small for her, and she could choke." On and on she went, claiming how she could use the money for other purchases that needed to be made. For all Connie knew, the woman had been given the item as a gift and was looking to make an easy buck. She continued to refuse the customer a refund until Lance suddenly appeared.

"Trouble, ma'am?" he inquired in his friendliest voice.

The customer explained the circumstances, all the while casting Connie a vicious look. Lance came around beside Connie, opened the cash register, and gave the customer her refund. The humiliation of it all irked Connie to no end, especially the smile Lance gave to the woman. Didn't he realize he may have just been duped?

"I was only adhering to company policy, Mr. Adams," Connie told him tersely, shoving the cash drawer closed with a resounding thud. "For all you know, that lady didn't even purchase the item here. She was just looking to make some easy money."

"Maybe so, but I want to keep customers not drive them away. So what's the matter? You aren't yourself at all. Get up on the wrong side of the bed this morning?"

Connie nearly told him about her run-in with Silas Westerfield but kept it buried within. If she did, no doubt he would hound her once more about giving up the clock. Instead, she looked away and helped another customer with a return item. During her morning break, Connie plunked herself onto the couch inside the lounge, wondering why she felt the way she did. The headache was driving her crazy, too.

Just then Lance appeared in the lounge to pour himself a cup of coffee. Connie wondered why management didn't have its own coffee for the offices. He added cream and sugar, slowly stirring the concoction together before his gaze settled on her.

"So what's going on, Connie?"

"Nothing. Have you ever had a bad day?"

"Plenty. But I don't think you're having a bad day here, are you?"

"Not here. It's just that my life seems to be going badly right now."

His facial features softened. "How so?"

"You would think it's silly. You're a guy. You wouldn't understand things like this."

"On the contrary, I have sisters. I understand more than you think."

"Really? How many?"

"Four. They're all older and married. I have four nieces and five nephews with number ten on the way. They have to remind me when their birthdays are. Too many to keep track of. And of course all my sisters are wondering when they're going to help plan their kid brother's wedding. In other words, they think I ought to get a move on."

Connie couldn't help marveling at the idea of Lance surrounded by women. That explained the pictures she saw in his office and the soft touch he had with everyone. No doubt older sisters were beneficial in his understanding of the female mind. How Connie wished she had sisters to confide in about her difficulties. Brothers had little sympathy for such things. They were creatures of fact not emotion. "That's funny, because I have two younger brothers."

Lance chuckled. "So then you must understand the male mind."

"You mean do I understand the colors of black and white, straightforwardness, without the emotional mushy stuff that gets in the way of the real facts? Yes, I suppose I do."

"At our house it was one big emotional party. Either the crying party or the happy-go-lucky, stay-up-all-night-and-chitchat party. I would have to go to Dad for a little male input at times." He cracked a grin and took a sip of his coffee. "Anyway, since I do have a little experience in dealing with women's problems, perhaps you can clue me in on yours. Unless it's personal or something, then I'll have to leave it alone."

"No, it's not personal. More spiritual, I guess. Honestly I don't even know what the trouble is." Her hand supported her chin as she paused in thought. "All I know is that I woke up with a weird feeling inside, like the peace of God just zoomed out of me overnight."

"Any particular reason?"

Connie refused to elaborate on the possible cause. She only said that things had been a little tight, and she found herself wishing that life could be easier to handle.

"We all go through that. The good old trials and tribulations. But God's Word is clear. 'Be of good cheer; I have overcome the world.'"

"I think it's more a matter of knowing His will," Connie said. "I have trials at times, but sometimes I think they come about because I don't know what He wants me to do."

"Have you asked Him?"

Connie straightened in her seat. The answer was so obvious,

she nearly gasped. "Asked Him? You mean pray?" When he nodded, she turned away before he could see her trademark flush creep into her cheeks. "I guess I haven't prayed about things like I should. I mean I do pray, but not consistently and certainly not about this situation since it blew up."

"One thing I've learned is that God is interested in everything we do in our lives. He wants to be involved. He wants to carry our burdens. But He can't do it if you don't allow Him to. And the way you allow Him is to put your cares on the altar of prayer. After that, He can tell you what to do—whether by the Bible, His still, quiet voice, or by way of other believers."

Lance spoke so matter-of-factly it was as if he had revealed the most common truth in the world, yet the words themselves were powerful. Of course as a Christian, Connie knew the necessity of prayer. Sometimes the situation clouded over her responsibility to seek peace and pursue it. Even now she had a peace over how to proceed, for which she thanked Lance.

He offered her a quick, "You're welcome," before disappearing to conduct his rounds of the store. Despite his heavy-handedness with regard to the clock, Lance had only been helpful with her situations. She thanked God for bringing the man to the store and into her life.

That evening Connie went to prayer over the clock, along with poring over the scriptures, hoping to hear the mind of God. Even with her own arguments in favor of keeping the timepiece, she couldn't get the picture of Silas Westerfield's sad face out of her mind. It was then that she came across the Gospel of Matthew. *"Give to the one who asks you, and do not turn away from the one who wants to borrow from you."*

Connie sucked in her breath as the words seemed to leap out at her from the pages. *Give to one who asks you. . . .* Could this be the word she should abide by? After all, didn't Silas Westerfield ask for the clock?

Connie slowly closed the Bible and gazed at the treasured timepiece. It would be difficult parting with it. She had to admit she had grown fond of the cuckoo popping out to greet her, even if it was a mechanical object made by man. The clock had become a part of her life. Just as Mr. Westerfield said, there was nothing like it in the world. But she also knew the clock couldn't become an idol either. She should be free to give it to whoever wanted it and feel no regrets. Besides the fact, there were plenty of other clocks available. She could still preserve the memory of long ago by purchasing a similar cuckoo clock while satisfying the desire of an elderly man at the same time. Connie nodded and closed the Bible. Tomorrow she would look up Mr. Westerfield's number and inform him of the good news.

❧

Connie was flipping through the phone book, looking for Silas Westerfield's number, when a knock came on her door. Peeking through the blinds, she found her neighbor, Claudia Rowe, standing on the step with a plate in her hand. Connie gasped in surprise. Claudia had never visited Connie, let alone spoken with her before the woman's recent yard sale, even though Connie had lived on West Street a few years. Like most people in the neighborhood, Claudia kept to herself. Occasionally Connie went out to greet the neighbors but found many of them indifferent or busy with their own lives, except perhaps for the McCalls who lived right next door to Claudia. She had often considered getting together a block party to meet more of the neighbors but never had the wherewithal to pull it off.

Connie opened the door with an enthusiastic greeting and invited her in.

Claudia smiled and stepped inside. In an instant, her gaze fell on the clock hanging on the wall. She inhaled a deep breath and ventured forward. "I made some cookies. I hope you like them."

"That's so thoughtful of you, Mrs. Rowe. How about I make up some tea?"

The older woman nodded and took a seat in the living room. Minutes later, with tea bags brewing in the cups, Connie ventured out to find her still looking at the clock. Were it not for the fact that Claudia once owned it, Connie would think she had the most unusual piece in the world with all the attention it wrought. She placed the cup on a coaster and settled in her seat. "How's the packing coming?"

"Oh, it's a lot of work," she confessed, dipping the tea bag in the hot water. "You find things tucked away in places you never knew existed. I'm amazed how much junk I've accumulated over the years."

Connie glanced around at her sparsely furnished apartment. That was one thing she never had to worry about—an overabundance of possessions. At least she was grateful for a roof over her head, even if the furnishings were old and a bit ratty-looking.

"I really should have one more sale before I move," Claudia continued.

"Well, I simply love the clock I bought at your last sale," Connie purred. Then it dawned on her that she had made the decision to sell the clock to Mr. Westerfield. She bit her lip, refusing to tell Claudia her plans and the money she would make in the venture.

"Actually, that's why I'm here." Claudia sat back in her seat and placed the cup on the table. "I wanted to make sure you were holding on to the clock."

"Holding on to it?" she said, her voice quaking. "Well, uh. . ."

"I put it in the yard sale in the hopes that whoever bought it would take care of it. And that means not reselling it. You understand, right?"

"I'm not sure I do."

"My dear, I'll be frank. There are some people in this world who would love to get their hands on this clock. But you must promise me you'll never sell it to anyone."

Connie blinked in astonishment. The seriousness of Claudia's request was plain to hear. It was almost as if the woman had an inkling she was prepared to sell it to Silas Westerfield. But how could she know? "I'm not sure what to say, Mrs. Rowe. I've bought plenty of items at yard sales, and yes, I have resold a few of them. I've never had anyone come to my door asking me not to sell something that's mine, though."

"I know, but this situation is unusual." She began twisting her fingers in obvious agitation. "Unfortunately there is one man in particular I don't want to have it. I saw him at the sale, you see. I was so glad you were interested in it. Quite frankly, if you hadn't given me the seventy-five, I might've let you take it for a lot less. Anything rather than letting that man have it."

Connie stared in bewilderment. "You mean you saw Mr. Westerfield at the sale?"

"You know him?"

"I don't know him personally, but yes, I've met him. And I

know he is very interested in the clock."

At that moment, Claudia jumped to her feet and began to pace. "This is what I was afraid of," she moaned. "I wish he would stop with this. What does it take to have my wishes followed?"

Connie could not believe it. Obviously at one time Silas Westerfield had been after Claudia Rowe about the clock, as he had with her. There seemed no limit to where the man might go with his interest. Were all antique dealers this nosy and determined to get what they want? "I'm sorry about this, Mrs. Rowe." Connie hastened to the bathroom to fetch a box of tissues.

Claudia Rowe dabbed her eyes. "I'm sorry you're caught in the middle of all this. I really thought I was doing the right thing by selling it. Now it seems I have to endure more heartache. I don't know when it will end either."

"It will end here," Connie said, unable to take the tears. "I'll keep it safe." She inhaled a deep breath. "It's strange you came when you did. I was getting ready to sell the clock to him. He offered me twelve hundred dollars for it."

Claudia Rowe nearly dropped the tissue. "Twelve hundred dollars!"

"Yes. It wasn't the money I was after, believe me. I just thought the clock was starting to become an idol of sorts in my life. I really loved it, as it reminded me of my grandmother's house and a difficult time that God saw me through as young girl. But I'm a Christian, you see, and I didn't want even a clock that served good memories to be a barrier in my life. A friend of mine at work encouraged me to pray about it. I did and decided after reading the Bible that it might be better to sell it since he seemed to want it so much."

"I hope after this I've managed to convince you otherwise."

"Is there—I mean is there something I need to know about this man? Is he a crook or something?"

"No, he's not a crook. He's. . ." She paused. "Let's just say he's been after my things before. He used to be poor, you know. I guess he thinks since I have such nice things he should be able to take them and resell them at his leisure."

"He doesn't seem poor," Connie observed. "Especially if he's able to offer that much money for a clock."

Claudia said little else. Connie could tell she was becoming more and more agitated by the meeting. In a way it reminded her of her grandmother when her ideas were questioned. Grandma would bristle, much like a cat when confronted in a corner without a means of escape. Angry words would come forth. Then Grandma would leave the room, followed by a slam of the door as a signature of her disgruntlement.

Again, the verse weighed heavily on Connie's heart. *"Give to the one who asks you."*

But two people have asked me for opposite things! What should I do?

"I didn't mean to upset you," Connie said. "Of course I will keep the clock. I only thought I was doing the right thing by getting rid of it. And he seemed to want it very much. He said there was nothing else like it in the world."

Claudia's face colored, but she said nothing. Instead, she grabbed her purse. "Well, I must be going. Thank you for the tea."

"Thank you for the cookies and. . ." Connie never finished her statement as Claudia Rowe exited her home in a flourish.

Connie sat still on the sofa, looking at the plate of oatmeal cookies and then at the clock that seemed to bring more trouble with each passing day. Maybe this was God's way of telling her to forget the yard sale scene. Maybe she was learning a valuable lesson through all this, not to buy things that could bring division among people. But then who would have thought a simple cuckoo clock could do such a thing? She had been to countless yard sales, bought things for herself and others, and never once found herself in the middle of a storm like this one.

There had to be a reason for it. God certainly knew what the clock meant to her. It was no mistake that she ran into Silas Westerfield not once but twice. And now Claudia Rowe had graced her doorstep for the first time. What could be the meaning behind it all? Would she ever learn the real answer before she became, as Donna suggested, kookier than the clock?

eight

Connie had to admit the encounter with Claudia Rowe left her feeling more confused than ever. As she lay awake that night, she wished she had never bought the clock. It had ushered in situations she never would have dreamed possible. And what made it all the more confusing was the assortment of people gravitating to the instrument. First there was Silas Westerfield, dressed in his trench coat, standing outside her front door and asking her to sell him the clock for twelve hundred dollars. Next came Lance, who all but ordered her to give in to Silas's request to sell the clock. Then there was Claudia Rowe, who had hardly ever spoken to her much less come to visit, arriving with a plate of cookies and begging her not to sell the clock to Silas under any circumstances.

Connie climbed out of bed and padded to the living room to gaze at the timepiece. How she wished the bird could speak to her, beyond those half-hour serenades alerting her of the time. She wished it could tell her why all these people were so interested in the clock while she remained in the dark. She thought she was doing the right thing by selling it so it wouldn't become an idol in her life. Just as she was prepared to do so, she was urged to keep it.

"God, I know Lance told me to come to You with my problems. I thought I had an answer to this mess, but I only seem to be growing more confused. Please show me what to do." She plopped down in the chair to ponder it all. She thought of asking the pastor of her church for advice, but wouldn't he think her troubles minor compared to the real problems of life? What if she went back and told Lance what Claudia had said? What kind of advice would he give? Connie wasn't sure she wanted his opinion. She had already found herself challenged by his suggestions in the past. She didn't think she could handle another round of rebuking, especially now.

A yawn nearly split her head in two. Connie wandered back to bed, knowing she had a full day of work tomorrow. Life was too short to worry about an old clock anyway. Unfortunately, that was exactly what was happening.

Connie arrived the next morning to find Sally asking if she had gone in search of the rocking chair like she'd promised. Connie told her not yet but that she would go soon. Inwardly she had already made up her mind that cruising yard sales just wasn't what it was cracked up to be, especially after this scenario with the clock. But she didn't want Sally to know this, as she had promised to search out a rocking chair for her mother's birthday. She moseyed on over to the customer service counter to find Donna already there, arranging the workstation for the day's influx of returns and other business. She was surprised to see Donna looking so organized. Ordinarily she was as messy as they come, especially when she had a sweet attack. Then the place would become saturated with candy wrappers and soda cans.

"Hey, long time no talk."

"Yeah," Connie said wearily. "It's been kind of hectic."

"Yeah? Like how?"

Connie wasn't certain whether to divulge her escapades concerning the clock and the people involved. After all, it was Donna who insisted she give in to the older man's offer in the first place. The clock meant little to her friend other than an item worthy of cold hard cash.

"C'mon," she coaxed. "I know I was a little heavy-handed about the clock, but I'm ready to listen and not jump to conclusions."

The statement surprised Connie. She sensed a bit of softening within Donna. She wondered if by some chance Lance had anything to do with it. Maybe he had taken Donna aside and talked with her. Connie saw him as a guy who could easily witness to the employees about God if the need arose. It would be an answer to her heartfelt prayer. At times Donna's opinions aggravated her to no end. Even though she knew Donna didn't have a relationship with Christ, Connie realized she needed to show Donna the same mercy God gave her whenever she made mistakes.

"Okay. I was all set to sell the clock like everyone was suggesting," Connie started. "I felt it was the best thing to do since I didn't want the thing ruining my life. Of course it still means a lot to me, especially with what it represents about my past and all. But if having the clock itself is causing things to go wrong in my life, then I thought it wise not to have it around. So I was all set to call Silas Westerfield when my neighbor stops in."

"Your neighbor?"

"Claudia Rowe. The lady I bought the clock from. She came knocking on my door, holding a plate of cookies and everything. I was pretty surprised to see her, considering we've hardly spoken to each other. I couldn't believe she was coming to my home for a visit. Of course, looking back on it, I should have invited her over a long time ago."

"So what did she want?"

"You won't believe this, but it seems like she found out that Silas Westerfield planned to buy the clock from me. She insisted that I not sell the clock to him or anyone else. She apparently believes she sold it to me on the condition that I would take care of it and not profit from it, so to speak."

"But it's your clock. You can do whatever you want with it."

Connie traced the smooth countertop with her finger. "I know. For some reason this clock is acting like a magnet, drawing people right to my doorstep. First it was Silas Westerfield. Then all the people at work wanted to see it. Lance has some kind of strange fascination with it. Now my neighbor. It's like this clock holds a secret."

"I think you're making mountains out of molehills."

"Maybe, but I know that an older lady, who has mostly kept to herself since she moved into the neighborhood, is now moving away, and a person like that doesn't suddenly start making house calls without a good reason. Don't you think it's strange?"

Donna smiled at a customer holding an active toddler who had come to return a toy she said had missing parts. "There's only one way to find out, Connie. Take the clock to a clock shop. There's a good one in Charlottesville. Maybe you'll find out it's actually some kind of rare antique worth thousands."

"More likely I'll end up right back where I started from."

Donna gave the woman her money then deposited the toy into the large plastic bin earmarked for toy returns. "If so, you're no worse off than you are right now. And if the clock isn't worth anything, then you can still sell it and make a little money."

"But I promised my neighbor I wouldn't."

Donna rolled her eyes. "Connie! Why did you promise her that?"

"She insisted that I keep it. I guess this man has been after her rare antiques in the past. She doesn't want him to get ahold of this clock. Believe me, she had the tears to go along with it. I can't stand seeing people cry, especially if I have anything to do with it."

Donna snickered. "Connie Ortiz—in the middle of a real mystery. Maybe you should go on one of those mystery shows."

"I just want my life back together," she said glumly.

"Cheer up. After work we'll check out that clock guy and see what the hubbub is all about. And if there isn't anything to this, then you can rest a little easier. At least you'll know you don't own a clock that once made Henry VIII happy."

"I don't think they had those kinds of clocks back then. I think they only began making them in Germany around two hundred years ago."

Donna patted her elbow. "I was just kidding."

The day went by slowly. Connie kept glancing at her watch, waiting anxiously for the shift to end so she and Donna could head right for the shop. She had already called the proprietor, and he agreed to give the clock a quick examination right after work. She would need to stop by the apartment and pick up the clock, then drive to Charlottesville in the hopes of finding the answers. There had to be a reason everyone was showing up at her place with an interest in this simple timepiece.

Near the end of the shift, Lance came over to check on the returns. When he saw Connie and Donna bustling about, he asked why they were in such a hurry.

"We have a very important errand to run," Donna told him. "We need to see if Connie struck gold."

Lance raised his eyebrows and glanced in Connie's direction. "If so, I hope she'll divvy it up with all of us. But I didn't know the Blue Ridge Mountains had gold."

Donna snickered. "No, we actually think there may be hidden gold inside the clock."

Lance stepped forward, intrigued. "Really now. And what makes you think that?"

"Why else would an old guy pay over a thousand dollars for it?" Donna took Connie's arm. "C'mon, we gotta get going."

Connie could clearly see the confusion painted on Lance's face but thought little of it. She and Donna headed right for her apartment. She managed to find the box for the clock while Donna raided the fridge for something to drink, complaining about the lack of food on the shelves. Once the clock was tucked away safely inside the box, they headed out. During the drive, Connie watched the splendor of the Blue Ridge Mountains in all its beauty rise up before her. The sight eased the misgivings about this whole venture. Donna chatted away about Connie's fame and fortune if she discovered that a clock bought at a yard sale was actually worth a huge sum of money. Maybe she would even be picked to do a talk show on bargain shopping. Connie only wondered what she would do after finding out the result of this visit.

They arrived at the Clock Shop in the downtown area. Hanging on the walls were clocks of every shape and size. From behind the counter, a small elderly gentleman ventured out, wearing magnifying spectacles. Connie noted in interest that he had a hook for one of his arms. She applauded the efforts of the man to do such delicate work, despite his physical challenge. He appeared like the perfect image of Geppetto from *Pinocchio*, but instead of puppets, clocks surrounded him.

"So this is the clock," he said when Connie opened the box. "Yes, indeed. An original Black Forest cuckoo clock. I recognize the workmanship."

Connie and Donna exchanged glances as the shopkeeper lifted the instrument out and set it carefully on the counter. Donna went on to tell the tale of the clock's past including the offer of twelve hundred dollars for it while Connie stood by.

The man carefully lifted off the front piece, using a fine whisk brush to dust away the dirt. "It's in excellent condition from what I can tell." He then turned it over, and with his magnifying spectacles, scanned the panel. "I assume you knew there's an engraving here on the back panel."

"What?" Connie leaned over the counter. The man brought out a magnifying glass so she could take a look. Even though the etching had faded with time, she could make out the words on the wooden panel. *Gene and Bette, 1960*.

"I wonder who Gene and Bette are?" Donna mused.

Connie shrugged. "Maybe Mrs. Rowe purchased it from either Gene or Bette. Is there anything else special that you can see about the clock besides the engraving?"

He looked it over. "It's a well kept instrument."

"It's very accurate," Connie added. "I wind it every eight days."

"I've seen many like it. While the age and condition of it would fetch a higher price, the engraving does lower the value. I don't believe it's worth much more than five hundred dollars." The man offered to keep the clock and give it a thorough cleaning, but Connie decided against it. Finances were tight enough as it was without having to pay a cleaning bill. She thanked him and returned the clock to its box before heading out the door with Donna.

"There, you feel better?"

"No. I feel worse. The only thing I know is that this is a nice clock with some kind of engraving on it from a previous owner. It doesn't explain why Silas Westerfield wanted to buy it for such a huge amount of money, or explain his claim that there's only one like it in the world." Connie sighed. "Oh, Donna, maybe you're right. Maybe I am making mountains out of molehills. Maybe I should just hang the thing on my wall and forget about it." But she knew she couldn't. This was not something easily forgotten. For a moment she could understand Claudia's exasperation with the thing and perhaps the reason why she had tucked it away in some obscure corner of the attic. Maybe she had found others wanting it because it was a treasured piece and then hid it away so as not to be reminded of it. Maybe that's exactly what Connie needed to do to restore the peace in her life—put the clock away for a time. Once the storms blew over, she could again have the clock gracing her living room wall.

Connie dropped Donna off at her apartment, thanking her for tagging along to the clock shop, then proceeded home. Her fingernails tapped on the box cover, the timepiece tucked away inside. "You're definitely full of mystery, Mr. Cuckoo," she murmured. "If only I had answers and not all these questions."

She pulled up to the apartment building to find a shadowy figure waiting on her doorstep, reading the evening newspaper. All at once a familiar dread came over her. At least this person wasn't wearing a trench coat. In fact, he looked vaguely familiar. In the lamplight she could see a crop of dark hair. He turned then and gave a friendly wave. Lance Adams.

Oh no. She glanced down at the clock sitting on the passenger seat of the car. She decided to leave the box inside the car and lock the car door. It made no sense to spark further discussion about the clock right now. Her head was already spinning.

"Hey, there," Lance said, folding the newspaper in half. "How's it going?"

"Okay," she said tentatively, wondering what the motive could be behind this impromptu visit.

"I'll bet you're wondering why I'm here."

No joke, she thought but offered a pleasant smile. "Are you homeless or something?" She grimaced at the remark. What an absurd comment to make—and with the connotation that he would seek refuge at her place.

He ignored it. "I was curious to know what happened with the clock."

I can't believe you came over here to talk about that clock, she thought in exasperation. How she wished he might pay *her* a little more attention. Or was he only paying her attention *because* of the clock? "I just wanted to make sure there was nothing strange about it, so I took it to a repair shop in Charlottesville."

"What do you mean? What's strange about it? Doesn't it work right?" The concern in his voice puzzled her.

"It's working fine," she said, wondering why he cared so much.

"Donna told me that Mrs. Rowe had asked you not to sell it."

When did Donna tell him that? "Yes, my neighbor did say that to me on her visit." She wished she could tell Lance that this was a private issue, and she would handle it. But for some reason the clock fascinated him, and she really wanted to know why. Could it be that Lance Adams had some kind of connection to it?

Suddenly she blurted out, "So why are you so interested in my clock, Lance? I've been wondering that for a long time. It can't be some passing fascination on your part. Most guys couldn't care less what's hanging on the wall. At least that's the way my brothers felt."

He stepped backward, as if her words had clobbered him. "Well," he began.

She tensed at his reaction.

"You could say that I'm also interested in the clock for personal reasons," he offered. "If you come with me to Luigi's, I'll tell you all about it."

The Italian restaurant that made her favorite pizza. He was making good on his promise to take her out for pizza, even if it did include conversation about the cuckoo clock. Connie smiled. No matter. She would enjoy a bite to eat and maybe in the process, find out a thing or two about Lance's connection to the clock. If only she were more of a gumshoe on par with Nancy Drew. Connie never felt she had the brains to solve a mystery, especially one involving herself. But a few clues would certainly do no harm—and maybe help her achieve that long-sought-after peace. "Okay. I am a little hungry."

His face relaxed, as if relieved she had accepted. They strolled along the sidewalk to where his car was parked. Connie looked back at her own vehicle and the clock sitting quietly on the front seat. What a web of a mystery the timepiece had weaved. She could hardly wait to discover the ending to it all, if she could make it there without going crazy.

nine

Connie wasn't certain what to think or believe as she sat in the passenger seat of Lance's immaculate car. The interior was clean as a whistle and smelled of polish, as if he had just spiffed it up at a car wash. The mere thought that he might have washed the car just for her sent tingles shooting down to her toes. She said little as they drove to the restaurant, making only casual comments about work. Lance then began chatting away about his first job as a grocery boy who delivered parcels to customers.

"And one time. . ." He began to laugh. Connie couldn't help smiling in return. Lance had a friendly, easygoing laugh that never failed to put her at ease. "I had two gallons of ice cream to deliver. This lady, Miss Paula we called her, loved her ice cream. Her tooth was sweeter than anyone I had ever met. I had the ice cream on the backseat, and before I could deliver it to her, my car had a flat tire. At the time, I was driving this really old rust bucket I affectionately called Rusty. In all honesty I was lucky to start it in the morning. So there I was in the middle of nowhere with two gallons of ice cream melting in the backseat. By the time I managed to get the tire changed, a glacial ice cream lake had formed on the seat and dripped to the floor. I called it Lake La Crème."

Connie laughed in glee. "Oh, Lance, you're hilarious."

He grinned. "So I had to run back to the store and tell Mr. Carson, the grocery clerk, what happened. Then I had to clean out my car. What a mess. And yes, you know what happens to milk when it sits awhile in a warm car."

"Ew!" she exclaimed, holding her nose.

"I never quite got the smell out after that. But Rusty was soon for the junkyard anyway."

"Lance, it's a good thing you're not telling me this story when we're about to eat or anything," she said with a wry grin.

Their lighthearted conversation instantly calmed her. Perhaps Lance realized her anxiousness when she first entered the vehicle. Like the good manager he was, he'd smoothed over the rough edges with a humorous tale about himself. She took it as a sign of a man who understood feelings, and like he claimed, one who grew up surrounded by the emotional complexities of women.

When they pulled into the restaurant lot, Connie was feeling much better and more confident—ready to face whatever Lance came here to discuss. She couldn't quite imagine what he might say. Right now the whole clock scenario was like a revolving door. Somewhere it had to stop. She prayed it would at the right entrance. When Lance held open the door for her and she gazed into his dark brown eyes, she wondered if perhaps the mysterious revolving door was meant to lead her to him. Maybe he was the one God had chosen to give her the answers.

Settling at their table, Connie immediately began giving the waitress an order for her favorite pizza with Italian prosciutto, black olives, artichokes, and Italian cheese. She then looked up into Lance's expectant face. "I'm sorry, I wasn't even thinking. I'm used to ordering the same pizza when I come here. Perhaps you want something else."

"Sounds good. I told you I wanted to try it sometime." He

added to the order two glasses of iced tea, then sat back expectantly with his arms crossed. "So how often have you eaten here?"

"A few times. Donna and I like it. She loves the atmosphere, the flowery curtains, the pictures of Italy on the walls." She pointed out the paintings. "She says that one day she would love to go over there and visit. Afterward, we head to the nearest video arcade."

"Really. She doesn't seem like the type who plays those kinds of games. I thought her pretty dignified, made-up—polished."

"Donna can be a little kid at heart when she wants to be. She likes to have fun, that is, when she's not bossing me around. I guess it's good though, since I don't have a sister. And she's been a great friend—even if she can be rather opinionated."

"But she isn't a Christian, is she?"

The drinks arrived. Connie poked a straw into the tea and took a sip. "No. I've talked to her some about it. Even tried to invite her to church. Once I was able to get her to go on an outing with the church ladies to that big outlet mall in northern Virginia. She had a blast, but she did say she was a little perturbed how everyone talked about God so much. I tried to use it as an occasion to say something about having a personal relationship with Christ. She thought it was strange."

"You did the right thing by inviting her along," Lance said. "You planted the seeds. We need to do more friendship evangelism nowadays. And I can tell you have a heart for it, Connie. It's no coincidence that you come from a background where families and friends join together to share meals and good times. We need to do more of that nowadays. We tend to shy away from it when it comes to these things. We're afraid to invite others into our world, afraid what they might think or how they'll react. But people are craving attention in their lives. They want five-star treatment. They want to know that others care about them. I hope maybe we can both begin organizing some of the events for the employees like I discussed awhile back."

Connie listened patiently, wondering if this was all a precursor to the conversation about the clock. Maybe Lance wanted to do more with the clock, like have another luncheon with coworkers. She sighed. And here she had been hoping to learn more details about the timepiece and especially Lance's involvement. Maybe there wasn't anything else to share. She grimaced in disappointment. Now she was right back where she started.

Lance gazed at her quizzically. "I guess you don't like my ideas?"

"Sure, it sounds great. I just thought we were going to talk about—oh, here's the food." The waitress arrived with the pizza. The aroma sent the juices swirling in Connie's mouth. At least her appetite hadn't been affected. It showed how comfortable Lance could make her feel, even if the conversation wasn't going the way she planned.

They both ate for a time, commenting every so often on the different kinds of pizza they had tried in the past, from a Philly cheesesteak variety to Hawaiian, barbecue, and even seafood.

"So did the clockmaker where you took the cuckoo say anything interesting about it?" Lance suddenly inquired.

Her stomach lurched. Luckily Connie had only eaten one slice of pizza when Lance popped the big question. So he had not forgotten the main crux of this outing. "He said it was in great condition."

"Did he say if he saw anything unusual about it?"

Connie coughed into her napkin. "Unusual? Like what?"

He waited patiently, as if expecting her to come out with it. Finally he said, "Like an engraving."

Connie stared in disbelief. How could Lance know so much unless Donna told him about the engraving? But she couldn't have. Lance was waiting at the front doorstep when she arrived home. Did he already have some preconceived knowledge of the clock then, as Connie had begun to suspect all along? "Yes, he said there was an engraving," she admitted. "I still don't understand how you would know about it, though. Maybe you can clue me in like you promised."

Lance picked up a napkin and began to fold it into a paper airplane. "It's pretty simple, Connie. The man who was trying to buy the clock from you—he's my grandfather."

Connie opened her mouth so wide she was sure he could see her tonsils. She clamped her lips together. "You mean that man in the trench coat is—I don't believe it. Silas Westerfield is your grandfather?"

"Yes, that's my granddad."

She sat stunned by the revelation, staring at the pizza slices before her. Now that her appetite had swiftly taken flight, there would be plenty of leftovers to take home.

Lance continued to fashion the airplane before resting it on the table. "And the engraving on it says '*Gene and Bette, 1960*,' right?"

Speechless, she could only nod.

"Gene is my grandfather," Lance explained. "It's his middle name. Silas Eugene Westerfield. He actually hated the name Silas. Everyone calls him Gene."

"No wonder he wanted the clock. Then why does Claudia

Rowe have it?" She paused. "Is she Bette?"

Lance winked. "You got it, lady. You're sharp. Yes, it was his nickname for her."

"And it must be that your grandfather gave her the clock. Now he's upset that she's parting with it, so much so that he's willing to pay an arm and a leg for it."

"Right again. At first I tried to talk Granddad out of it. I said how you were my employee at work and had really taken a liking to the piece. Granddad agreed at one time to leave it alone, but I guess he changed his mind. I know he's asked a few times about it. He mentioned how you gave him a ride home the other day. That was really kind of you, Connie."

"Now everything he said to me makes sense, especially the comment that there's no other clock like it in the world. So he had the clock engraved for Bette?"

"It was an engagement gift of sorts. A gift of promise. They both loved antiques. I don't know if you've seen the inside of Mrs. Rowe's house, but she's quite a collector. That's how they first met, you know. At an antique store over in Fredericksburg. They were both living in this area at the time. Virginia is an antiquer's paradise, you might say.

"As a promise of a future life together, Granddad bought her the clock as a gift. Not long after, a few months maybe, they broke off their engagement and Bette moved away. Granddad never really told me why they parted. But he always wondered about her and what happened. I'm sure when she moved back into the area a few years ago he wanted to open up communication. By that time Grandma was dead. I think Bette had lost her husband as well. But Granddad was never one for chasing women. He's a gentleman. He had hopes Bette might want to see him. She never did. And when he saw her selling the clock at the yard sale, he knew she meant to erase any memory of what they once had long ago."

"How tragic!" Connie moaned. "Your grandfather and Mrs. Rowe engaged in a lover's quarrel."

"I can't say that he loves her now. They probably did love each other at one time. Now he simply wants the clock back. He believes it's his after it was given out of a promise. When that promise was broken, he felt he should have had it returned. And I think he saw his opportunity when a nice young lady purchased the clock at the yard sale."

"Of course I'll return the clock to him." She paused. "Oh no. I promised Claudia I would keep it. Wow, now everything she said on her visit makes sense. She said this elderly man wanted the clock really bad; that he was after her priceless objects or something to that effect. She made your grandfather sound like a crook. She sat in my apartment and shed tears about it all. After all that, Lance, I promised her I wouldn't sell it."

Lance blew out a sigh. "Then I guess Granddad will have to accept it. At least he can find comfort in knowing the clock is in good hands." Just then he leaned over and grasped Connie's hand. "And speaking of hands, I must confess that I've wanted to hold yours for quite a while. You have such long, lean fingers. I notice them while you're working at the customer service desk. But holding hands isn't quite what a manager and an employee should be doing."

A buzz like a bee filled her ears. Warmth flowed through her. Here they had been discussing a love that was lost, and now a new love was blossoming in its place.

He released her hand to take up the airplane he had made out of the napkin. "So I guess we're going to have to let this go, aren't we?" He held up the paper plane, preparing to fly it across the restaurant.

"Don't you dare let that go," she said with a giggle. "You'll cause a stir! Anyway, it doesn't necessarily mean we have to let your granddad and Claudia go their separate ways. If there's anything left from the past, maybe we can coax it along a little."

"And just how do you plan to do that?"

"At one time Bette and your grandfather were in love. They had to be if they were engaged and your grandfather bought her a clock with their names engraved on it. It's just like lovers who engrave their names on a tree. After all that, I think we should see if there might be some sparks left from long ago. I'm sure there is."

"I'm not so sure, Connie. It sounds to me like whatever argument they had left scuff marks on their hearts."

"Then we need to buff up those hearts a little. We need them to shine once again. The Bible says to be reconciled. We need to see that this couple is given the opportunity to do just that. Who knows? Maybe other fruit will happen, too."

"You're incredible, you know that? Granddad was fortunate to have that clock fall into your hands. It was definitely no accident that you love yard sales and that clock caught your eye."

Connie smirked, realizing she had been thinking the same thing. For a time she thought the clock might well be a curse that brought tribulation to her life. Now that she had learned the story, how the clock served as a link between two young people who were once in love, it took on a greater meaning. Perhaps it might bring the relationship back to life. "Only time will tell," she murmured.

"What?"

Connie confessed to him the play on words she had devised, to which he laughed.

"I don't think you're too far off. It would be nice to see them reconcile after all these years, and especially since they're both lonely people."

"Does your grandfather ever talk about Claudia or Bette, I guess is her name?"

"A few times since Grandma died ten years ago. That's how I found out about the clock and the engraving. That's not to say Grandma's passing wasn't hard on Granddad. He loved her very much. They did everything together. When he broke his hip, she stayed by his side constantly."

"Is that why he walks with a limp?"

"Yes. He broke it eleven years ago. One leg is shorter than the other. All he needs to do is get a shoe built up, but he isn't fond of doctors or the way they do things. He believes the doctors messed up his leg to begin with. So he's gotten used to walking with a limp. Sometimes he uses a cane, but he hates it. Says it makes him look old. When I told him he *was* old, you should've seen the look I got!"

Connie snickered. "He talked about how the family made comments concerning his trench coat."

Lance nodded. "Another testy subject. I did talk to him a little about his taste in clothes. He's fairly set in his ways. That's why I don't see much coming from a reunion between Granddad and Mrs. Rowe. He knows it's been a long time, and they are different people. I'm sure they will be polite to each other, but that's about as far as it's likely going to go."

"We can at least try. It can't do any harm. After all, God has unique ways of bringing people together. I mean, look at how we're sitting here talking about a clock I bought at a yard sale. That little cuckoo bird is being used in more ways than one."

Lance stood to his feet and left some bills on the table. "This has been fun, Connie. I'll have to admit, at first I dreaded this meeting. I know you weren't too happy about my involvement with your clock. When this all came up, I debated telling you right off that Mr. Westerfield was my grandfather. Somehow I didn't feel comfortable about it until I knew you better and could gauge your response."

Connie dropped her head, realizing how her attitude had affected the situation. If she hadn't been so vexed about his involvement, she would've had the answers to her troubles a lot sooner. She was thankful the clock's magnetism had drawn them together for a special purpose. "I'm really sorry how I came off at first. I was deep into my own personal feelings and still am, I guess. But I must admit I find this scenario between Claudia and your grandfather to be quite intriguing. I'd like to see this cuckoo clock bring them back together. It will make all the trouble worth it and more."

They strode out of the restaurant toward the car. Above them a crescent moon shone overhead. It was a perfect spring evening, despite the slight chill in the air. Lance opened the passenger door for her, and soon they were on their way down the dark road. Connie sat huddled in her seat, reminiscing about the evening, wishing it didn't have to end so quickly. Though she needed to work tomorrow, Connie knew sleep would be slow in coming tonight. "Do you think it would be all right if I did a little probing?" she inquired. "Maybe ask Claudia Rowe a few questions and uncover some clues about their past relationship?"

"As long as it doesn't upset her. I'd proceed with caution. Maybe once you find out a few tidbits we can figure out where to go from there."

Connie nodded, excited at the possibility, when Lance pulled up to her apartment. He waited for her to enter the dark apartment before driving off. She flicked on a light, only to find the clock missing from the wall. Panic assailed her until she remembered the clock was still inside her car on the dark street. The wall seemed empty without the merry piece to entertain her. If all this worked out and Bette or Gene decided they wanted their clock back, Connie knew she must be ready to part with it. The clock had once knit two young lovers together until some kind of misunderstanding forced them apart. She would like nothing better than to see them reunited, even if it did cost her the most prized object she had ever purchased.

ten

Connie didn't want to admit it, but she was nervous about the meeting with her neighbor. She spent much of the morning rehearsing what she might say so Claudia wouldn't become angry. It was a risky endeavor, she knew, but worth it if by some chance God might be knitting this long-lost couple back together. Mixed in with all of this were her strong feelings for Lance. She recalled with pleasure the warmth and strength of his hand on hers during dinner at the restaurant. At first the contact startled her. She had always found Lance a strong and attractive Christian man, but it didn't dawn on her that he might also be attracted to her. Now she considered their various interactions over the past few weeks. He met up with her almost daily in the store, accompanied by a friendly word or greeting. At first she assumed it was a part of normal managerial relations. Now she wondered if there were other reasons behind the communications. Of course they had a link with the clock. She owned the very piece that could unite his grandfather with the woman he would have married had they not broken their engagement. Yet there was also sincerity in Lance's gaze during dinner and the way he commented about her hands. It led her to believe his interest extended far beyond business and a simple wooden cuckoo clock to something much more personal.

For now Connie put Lance's interest on the back burner to focus on the encounter with Claudia. She had walked by the home earlier that morning to find boxes strewn across the front porch. No doubt her neighbor was in the midst of packing. Perhaps Connie should make a visit on the guise of offering some assistance with the packing, along with returning the plate that once held the delicious oatmeal cookies. There was no better opportunity than using the ministry of a servant's heart to bring forth a topic of deep importance. Connie had done such things with others on numerous occasions, including Donna. While the person sometimes didn't always respond the way she had hoped, at least it provided an avenue in which to tackle difficult subjects.

Just then the phone rang. Connie hurried to answer it as the cuckoo on the wall interrupted with a cheery greeting.

"I can hear the clock," Lance said with a chuckle. "It must be a sign."

"It's been a sign ever since I bought it. Every half hour on the half hour."

"Connie, it was a sign long before you bought it. And I'm hoping it might bring happiness into two people's lives. That's why I'm calling, to wish you faith and grace on your visit with Mrs. Rowe. Have you thought about what you want to say?"

"A little. Actually, I decided just to make myself useful and hope the words will come out. She has a bunch of boxes on her front porch, so she's probably hip-deep into packing."

Lance blew a sigh over the phone. "I hope we aren't too late. Once she moves away, that's it. Granddad won't track her down. I know it. He won't interfere with her plans. We need to do something as soon as possible."

"I have to say I'm a little anxious about the meeting. We could be setting ourselves up for a big fall if something goes wrong."

"It won't."

"Easier said than done. It seemed like a good idea, too. I guess I'm getting cold feet."

"Then warm them up a little. Confess some good scripture like, 'I can do all things through Christ who strengthens me.' I don't think it's an accident that you live a few doors down from the woman my grandfather once loved. When I saw Granddad other day, I could tell he'd been thinking about the past. He had a note with Bette's old address on it lying on his desk. I asked him about it, but he only put it away and said nothing. If you could see the longing in his eyes, Connie, it would give you the strength to go forward with this, as uncomfortable as it might seem."

"I believe you. Just pray for me, and we'll see what happens. And maybe in the meantime you can work a little more on your grandfather. Maybe encourage him to give Mrs. Rowe a call. Something to open up the doors of communication."

"Sounds good. Talk to you later."

Connie hung up the phone, breathing a sigh of relief. As was his nature, Lance had instilled in her a confidence she sorely lacked. She picked up her purse along with the plate that Claudia had used to bring over the cookies, took one last look in the mirror, and made for the door. She breathed a prayer for God's will to be done.

❧

Claudia Rowe greeted Connie with a surprised look when she opened the door. Her hair was bound up in the turban she'd worn at the yard sale. Tiny beads of perspiration dotted her forehead. "Oh, my plate," she said when she saw the dish in Connie's hands. "Thank you for returning it. I nearly moved away without it."

"Looks like you're packing," Connie observed, acknowledging the open boxes and the dishes Claudia had just begun to wrap in tufts of paper.

"Yes, and it's hard work, I must admit."

"I'd be glad to give you a hand. I can wrap the dishes, and you can pack them."

"Well. . ." She seemed to consider the offer while scanning the many dishes on the counter. "All right, but please be careful. Many of these are antiques."

"No problem. When my grandmother had to move, I helped pack up her antiques. She had quite a few in a display case. And many Hummels as well." Connie took up a sheet of paper and began wrapping a glass. "I loved this one Hummel she had of a little girl holding an umbrella. She had such a sweet expression on her face, as if wondering whether the umbrella would protect her from the storm."

"Is your grandmother the one who owned a cuckoo clock?"

Connie nodded, placing the glass carefully in a cardboard box half full of Styrofoam peanuts. "She had quite a few antiques. I was grateful to get this one piece before it all went to auction. A little pink glass slipper with gold etching."

Claudia Rowe glanced at her in curiosity. "A glass slipper! It sounds like something from *Cinderella*."

"I always thought I would turn into a princess if I could get my foot into it," Connie reminisced with a laugh. "Unfortunately, it was the size of a toddler's shoe. And I was about five or six at the time. Still I don't have very big feet even as an adult."

"You're quite petite," the woman observed. "You look a lot like my youngest daughter, Karen. That's where I'm moving, near where my two daughters live. They both live in Virginia

Beach. I'm not getting any younger, you know. I want to be close to them and their families. One of my grandsons is getting ready to graduate from high school. Can you believe it?"

"You don't look old enough to have grandchildren that age! I think it's a great idea, though. It would be wonderful living near the ocean, watching the waves roll in and seeing the sun rise in the morning." Connie wrapped up a few more pieces, all the while wondering how to broach the subject concerning Lance's grandfather. It appeared Claudia had her heart set on moving near her family. Obviously Silas Westerfield was nowhere in the picture. She continued on with small talk about her grandmother's house and some of her antiques. "You have quite a collection here."

"Yes, many years' worth. I really should just get rid of it all, but it's difficult. Some of the pieces are very old. A few I collected pretty near forty years ago."

"Really. I'll bet the clock I have was one of them, huh?"

Claudia paused. Her hand jerked as if Connie had touched a nerve. "Not really. The clock was given to me."

An open door! Connie decided to pounce on it before it slammed shut in her face. "It must be a secret admirer, then. Or else the clock did have some other kind of secret between two people."

"I'm not sure what you mean."

"I had it looked at by a clock repair shop in Charlottesville. The man there discovered an engraving on it." Connie turned to look at her. The color had drained away from the older woman's face, leaving it white like the petals of an Easter lily.

"Well, it doesn't mean anything," she declared.

"The shopkeeper told me it said, *Gene and Bette, 1960.* I'm guessing someone else had it before you did?"

Just then a teacup slipped out of Claudia's hand and crashed to the linoleum in a million sharp shards. "Oh, look what happened!" she cried.

"I'm sorry. Where's the broom? I'll clean it up."

Claudia ignored her request and hunted down the broom and dustpan herself. With methodical strokes, she began sweeping it up. "I only have two of these left now," she moaned. "They were original cups from my wedding china. I don't know, but in the last few years I've had wedding china breaking right and left. Now I only have a few pieces left."

Connie didn't know what to say. The pitiful look Claudia gave was enough to make her want to share in the tears that came trickling down the older woman's face. This visit may well have already turned into a dreadful mistake.

Claudia now took a seat on the sofa. "My Herbert died ten years ago from colon cancer. When the doctors found out about it, they didn't treat it until it was too late. He should have never died at such a young age."

"I'm so sorry for your loss."

"We had a wonderful marriage. He was a lovely man, just the man Daddy wanted me to marry. And I was glad I did, of course." She seemed lost in thought.

"Is he. . .I mean, did he give you the clock?"

"Oh, no. That came from someone else. Someone before Herbert. Someone who is trying to come back, even though I want him to stay away. What we had was so long ago. We both took different paths in life. I wish he would accept it."

Connie stood still, her heart pattering away, hoping and praying she would continue.

"It wasn't that Gene was a bad man. Just the opposite. He was sweet and kind, but my family was suspicious of him. He was poor, and I was the daughter of a wealthy businessman. Daddy always wanted me to marry the vice president of his company. They thought Gene was a street urchin trying to wheedle his way into the family fortune. But he was wonderful to be around." She reached over to grab a tissue out of a box. "We had a lot in common, too. We both loved antiques. Gene was a whiz at finding antiques and getting the best deals. I told him he should become a dealer. We would browse through all kinds of shops. He could negotiate the most wonderful bargains. I really did love him." She paused. The lonely sound of the grandfather clock serenaded the moment.

"Then one day Gene bought me the cuckoo clock. He had seen me looking at it in one of the shops. He brought it over to my parents' house when they weren't home. He said it was an engagement gift, a promise that we would always be together. 'As time endures so will our love' he told me." She blew her nose. "Isn't that romantic?"

"Yes, it is." Connie tried to imagine Silas Westerfield, outfitted in his trench coat, saying such things under the faint rays of moonlight. No doubt he was a dashing man with a romantic heart, and still was to have a grandson that followed suit.

"He showed me the engraving he had put on the clock. I was so touched. Oh, I did want to be with him, I must admit. But when Daddy found out that Gene was serious about marrying me, my parents did everything they could to keep us apart. Daddy went so far as to send a person to spy on him. He discovered that Gene's brother was a swindler and believed Gene was the same way. I knew Gene didn't have a lot of money. He had no nice clothes. He drove a lemon of a car that always seemed to break down—and at the most inopportune times. He rarely had money to take me out."

Connie winced when she heard how Silas Westerfield's financial status had cast a pall over their relationship. She certainly hoped such things would not hinder her relationship with Lance, even if her own finances weren't as stable as she would like.

"At first the money didn't matter. But Daddy was insistent. He said Gene was after our fortune. He wasn't a good man for me. Eventually I believed him. Why wouldn't a daughter believe that her father had her best interests at heart? So I told Gene we couldn't get married. Without my family's blessing, there was no hope for us anyway. There would always be contention and resentment somewhere, and I didn't want to live like that. Gene refused to accept it. He said we could elope. We were meant to be together. But I wouldn't. I was my father's girl, and I would honor his decision."

Claudia began to cough then and went out to the kitchen to pour some filtered water into two glasses. She returned, handing one to Connie. "I said to Gene it would be better if we stopped seeing each other. Not long after that we went our separate ways. I took the clock with me, as I did like it very much. Gene tried to contact me on several occasions, but Daddy told him to leave us alone or face the consequences. Gene stayed away after that. We lost track of each other. Then I found Herbert, a coworker in the company. Daddy highly approved of him. He was a nice man and gave me everything I wanted. But I must admit, deep down in my heart, I never forgot Gene or the clock he gave me, even if I kept it hidden away in the attic all these years."

Connie could hear the wistful tone in her voice, of one who wished circumstances might have played out differently. Of course she was glad it hadn't, for Lance wouldn't be here. Still

God had a way of orchestrating events in people's lives, even years later. "It's not too late for you and Gene," she told Claudia.

"I'm afraid it is. We both went in different directions. I found a husband. Gene found a wife. We raised families, and now we both have grandchildren."

"His grandson believes it isn't too late."

Claudia looked at her quizzically. "You act as if you know who Gene is?"

"I do, Mrs. Rowe. I know that Gene is really Silas Westerfield, the one who wanted to buy the clock from me."

Claudia gasped. "Don't tell me he dragged you into this mess! How could he do such a thing?"

"He didn't say a word about this to me. His grandson, Lance, is the assistant manager at the store where I work. We've come to know each other pretty well. He recently told me how Mr. Westerfield bought you the clock as an engagement gift."

"Why he wants it returned to him after all these years, I have no idea. I can't believe he suddenly cares about it."

"He must care if he's willing to offer twelve hundred dollars for it. Or maybe he cares about the owner and feels the clock is the best way to reach her heart."

Claudia shook her head. She stood up and returned to wrapping up the dishes. "What we had died a long time ago. He shouldn't try to resurrect something that never was and never will be. And to think he tried to get it from you by offering such a huge amount of money."

"I think it's sweet."

Claudia cast her a look that sent a chill racing through her.

"I mean it's obvious he wants to communicate with you again. But he's a gentleman and doesn't want to seem as if he's interfering."

"He is interfering by wanting something that can never be. It's over. No clock will bring it back."

"Is it really over? You even said at one time you wanted to be with him. There must have been something there between you two. The years don't have to erase it."

Claudia stood still as if stunned by the words. Connie watched the lines of aggravation break out across her face. She said no more and helped finish packing up a box. Once it was filled, Claudia taped it up.

"I think we're done for today," she announced. "I can tell that you came over here to try to arrange something between Gene and me. I'm sure his grandson helped, too."

"I only thought that maybe after all these years there might be something left of a young couple who was once in love. And I know you both were in love. I could hear it in your voice and see it in your face."

Claudia winced and turned away. "Thank you for your help. I should be able to finish this myself."

Connie reluctantly picked up her purse and moved toward the door. She wanted to say more but bit her tongue. She had said too much already. At least she was thankful her neighbor had revealed a few facts to her. If only there weren't such barriers existing between Claudia and Lance's grandfather. If this was indeed a match that could transcend time, was it possible for Lance and her to bring it to pass? Both Gene and Bette had families, children, and grandchildren. And forty years was a long time. But there must be some spark left, even if Claudia's family had tried to smother it. Perhaps a breeze of opportunity might fan the flames. If only she knew what the next step should be—or if there was a next step, whether it should be hers.

eleven

"Why didn't you answer your phone last night?" Lance inquired as soon as Connie dropped her purse inside the employee locker. "I nearly drove over to your house to ask what happened, but I managed to restrain myself."

Connie knew he had called. His number flashed on the caller ID. Yet she couldn't bring herself to answer the phone after the encounter with Claudia Rowe. She was grateful the woman had opened up about her life, but the avenue to Silas Westerfield appeared closed with the detour sign reading VIRGINIA BEACH. Her neighbor was determined to move. She had given the clock into Connie's care with the hope of sealing shut the past. Connie felt if she pursued it any further, she would be setting herself up for a big fall.

Lance peered at her intently before pouring a cup of coffee. "I guess it didn't go very well."

"I learned quite a bit, but I don't think this is worth pursuing. From Claudia Rowe's standpoint, she believes they took separate paths, then got married and had families. It's those families they should look to now, not some long-lost love of decades ago."

Lance's face twisted in obvious disappointment. He opened his mouth, ready to speak more, when Donna came bopping in. "Hey, you two!" she said with a shrill. "So how was the date the other night?"

"Date?" Connie asked blankly.

112

Lance excused himself and headed out the door. Donna looked at her quizzically. "Wow, must have been a bummer."

"If you mean the pizza, that part went fine. It was the conversation surrounding it."

Donna groaned. "Connie, you're going to have to quit with your opinions and lighten up a little. So did you sit there and tell Lance what to do with the store?"

"No. And don't try to guess either. You'll never even scratch the surface."

Donna stepped closer, the challenge igniting a fire in her eyes. "Just try me."

"Okay. You know that older man who wanted to buy the clock?"

"Of course."

"He's Lance's grandfather."

Donna's mouth fell open, exposing the gum she had been snapping. "No way." She pressed her lips together and began to chew.

"Yes, and that's not all. My neighbor who sold me the clock, Mrs. Rowe—it turns out she and Lance's grandfather were once engaged to be married. The clock happened to be a gift he bought for her."

"So the engraving that said Gene and Bette?"

"Gene is Silas Westerfield's middle name. And Bette was his nickname for my neighbor."

"This is too wild to believe! Our manager is the grandson of Gene? Wowsie. No wonder the man was so interested in your clock. This couldn't get any stranger."

"So now Lance and I are trying to think of a way to get them back together after all these years."

"Wouldn't that be sweet! I guess they're both widowed?"

"Claudia Rowe lost her husband to cancer. I'm not sure how Lance's grandmother died. He never told me. But Claudia said at one time she cared a lot for Gene. There must be some kind of feelings left, even if she's denying it."

Donna took a seat at the table and cupped her face with her hands. "So what exactly do you plan to do? Give me all the juicy details."

"There's nothing much happening right now. She got angry when I told her that Gene must still care about her if he was trying to buy back the clock after all these years. She saw no connection but only pronounced the relationship dead in the water."

"You need to coax the two of them along a little. Look at the success I had with you and Lance!" Donna winked.

Connie stepped back. "You didn't have anything to do with us. I mean, Lance and I just started talking. It's true you first mentioned him to me. When you think about it, though, that clock also brought us together."

"So what's the next step?"

"Right now there isn't one."

"Honey, there's always a step to be made. You need to come up with a way for the two of them to meet face-to-face. Think of a common interest they share."

Connie paused to consider this. Donna seemed gung ho over the idea of uniting the older couple, despite what happened with Claudia. If only she could be certain about what to do. There were no manuals in this area but biblical guidance. And there it said to live peaceably with all men and above all, to trust God. Maybe in His own mysterious way, having Donna enter the picture might create a path between Gene and Bette, if that were possible.

"They both like antiques," Connie suddenly declared. "That's the whole reason Gene gave her the clock in the first place. And she loved it from what she told me. When they went their separate ways, she kept the clock hidden until the yard sale where I bought it."

"Then maybe you can arrange to have them meet at an antique market. That seems the most logical place. It's worth a try." Donna hopped to her feet, gave a wave, and took off.

Connie puzzled over the suggestion in light of the visit she had just made with her neighbor. It seemed harmless enough, arranging for the couple to meet at an antique market. There was a nice one out on Highway 29. She could ask Claudia to go with her one Saturday, perhaps on the notion of needing advice on old rockers for Sally's mother. Nodding her head at a possible game plan, Connie made for the customer service desk.

The workday passed by without any major shake-ups, for which Connie was grateful. To her surprise, there was no sighting of Lance all day. After the plans they had made, she was certain he would appear at various times to talk about what happened. Even at lunch he was nowhere to be found. Rumors soon spread of high-level business meetings within the store management. She could picture him sitting tense at the meetings, his personal data assistant in hand ready to take notes, a silk tie hanging loose around his neck, the sleeves of his white cotton shirt rolled to the elbows, his dark eyes alert. The mere thought of him made her tingle. She glanced down at her right hand, the one he held that night at the restaurant. There must be something brewing between them for her to feel the way she did, and for him to hold her hand on their first outing together.

Just then a deliveryman appeared at the customer service

counter. "I'm looking for a Constance Ortish."

"Ortiz," she corrected, staring in surprise at the basket filled with a variety of spring flowers, from daisies to tulips to the heavenly scent of hyacinths that filled her head with a sweet fragrance.

The man left the basket on the desk. Donna immediately bounced over and took the card. "I bet I can guess who sent this."

Connie thought she could, too, even as her fingers shook while opening the envelope.

> *Thanking you for your kindness.*
> *Silas Eugene Westerfield*

Donna repeated the simple message. "Wow! It wasn't who I thought. Hey now, if that isn't a go-ahead to try to bring them together, I don't know what is! Reading between the lines, I'd say he's thanking you for helping him and Bette out."

"But I haven't done anything," she said. "And I refused to sell him the clock."

"Lance probably told him how you talked to Bette, and he's thanking you for it. That means he wants to get back together with her."

"I suppose it does. Maybe this is the sign I've been waiting for." She touched one of the soft tulip heads then inhaled the fragrance of the hyacinth.

Just then Lance appeared. Seeing him, Donna shot Connie a quick smile before busying herself with sorting out returns.

"So they came," Lance observed. "Granddad said he was going to send you something. I told him it wasn't necessary, but he wanted to."

"They're lovely. Does this mean he's giving us permission to try to work things out between himself and my neighbor?"

"He won't do it himself, so I guess we should take up the torch. How about we grab some food for a picnic and meet at the park? We can talk over a game plan there."

"That would be nice."

"Good. See you after work." He waltzed away, whistling a tune as if happy about the plan.

Donna gave her a thumbs-up signal. "Looking good. Our manager is falling head over heels in love. Like grandfather, like grandson."

Connie wasn't certain she would categorize their relationship in that light, but at least she was spending more time getting to know Lance. She sailed through the last remaining hour of the workday, all the while anticipating the picnic that evening. After the work shift ended, she headed home to dress in something more comfortable and give a drink of water to the pretty arrangement of flowers. She wondered if Silas Westerfield really did send the flowers or if Lance did it in disguise. Whatever the reason, Connie enjoyed how the arrangement spruced up her apartment.

When Mr. Cuckoo emerged for his five o'clock serenade, she lifted up the basket of flowers. "All this is because of you," she informed the famous clock. "Not only do I get a basket of sweet-smelling posies but also an outing with a wonderful guy."

Just then she heard the sound of a car. Glancing out the window, she saw Lance approaching the door. "Sorry I didn't tell you specifically where and when to meet," he said, digging his hands into the pockets of his jeans. "We can make a stop at a deli and grab something to eat."

"I'll be ready in a minute." She ran around breathless, fetching her purse and some paper products left over from the luncheon. It had been a whirlwind of an invite, but she was looking forward to sharing about his grandfather, Claudia Rowe, and tidbits about themselves. When she returned, Lance held the door open for her. The sky was an azure blue, the birds active as they fluttered about, even with the sun dipping low on the horizon. It was a perfect evening to have dinner and talk beneath a canopy of trees.

ఇ

The picnic was a great success. With Connie's disposable dishes and the food Lance had purchased at the deli—including a rotisserie chicken and potato salad—it couldn't have been better. They chatted for a time about the store. Lance mentioned how he might be away next month to help start a sister store over the mountain in the valley. Connie marveled at the responsibilities he had been given, wondering why he would want to associate with someone of her status. None of it seemed to matter to him, though, as he delved into the main topic of their get-together—Gene and Bette.

"When I talked to you earlier, you didn't seem too thrilled over the meeting you had with your neighbor."

Connie nodded. "She wasn't thrilled at all. In fact, she was pretty upset, so I didn't want to press the issue."

Lance considered this. "I tried talking with Granddad about her. He didn't say much. In fact, he never really told me why they broke off their engagement. Not that I'm upset about it— I wouldn't be here if they had married!" He cracked a grin.

"That's true. I guess we need to be thankful that it didn't work out. When Mrs. Rowe told me what happened, though, I'll have to say it was pretty sad."

Lance leaned forward, his eagerness for information spelled out in his eyes that reflected the coming twilight. "What happened?"

Connie proceeded to tell him of the falling out they had because of the differences in their social status. "It's sort of like us—hypothetically, I mean—you're a guy with a great and wonderful career, and I'm just a little old clerk behind a desk."

"Connie, we're people. . .not items to be compared with on a store shelf. Anyone who puts a price tag on a human being is crazy."

"I think that's what happened with Claudia and your grandfather. Claudia's father told her she couldn't marry him, and she abided by his wishes. They ended up moving away. She lost contact with your grandfather after that."

"Poor Granddad. At least he did find someone else in my grandmother. She died ten years ago."

"So did Claudia Rowe's husband. Of cancer."

"Same with my grandmother. Strange coincidence. And now we have two lonely people who were once engaged, trying to find their place in life."

"Claudia feels her place is with her daughters in Virginia Beach. I don't think your grandfather is anywhere in the equation. But I'm wondering if perhaps something can still be done. It's obvious your grandfather cares a great deal about her. I don't think he would have sent a basket of flowers to thank me if he felt I was doing something wrong."

"You're right about that."

Connie gazed up into the tree branches. It was a perfect place for a picnic, right beside the glistening waters of a gurgling brook. "We need to find a way for them to meet. Donna suggested we try to bring them together using some common interest. Since they both love antiques, maybe we can use that area. In fact I was thinking of that nice antique center out on Highway 29."

"Hmm. A possibility. Granddad likes going there. I wouldn't have any trouble coaxing him to come. But what about you? How do you plan to get Mrs. Rowe there? I'm sure she's plenty busy with moving and all."

Connie traced the back of the park bench with her finger. "I have an idea. Sally wants a rocking chair. I'm hoping Claudia can lend me a hand deciding which style chair might be suitable. Sally wants me to find one at a yard sale, but I can still look around at an antique place, too."

"You've got the brains to match your looks," Lance said.

Connie gazed at him in wonder. To her delight, she found him staring at her with a look she couldn't decipher. How she wished she could read his mind. Did he truly like what he saw? Her question was answered when he scooted over ever so slowly and curled his arms around her, ushering her toward him. The next moment, Connie was experiencing the warmth of his lips and the fragrance of his cologne washing over her. A bird landed on a limb just above them to serenade the moment with a song. Lance pulled back and chuckled.

"Maybe that was a song of approval," he said softly.

"I don't know, Lance. I'm not sure."

He straightened as if he had been reprimanded. "I'm sorry, Connie. I thought maybe you—I guess I read this wrong. Sorry."

"What do you mean? I was thinking about how to get Claudia to go antique shopping with me." She giggled at the confusion that distorted his features. "Anyway, I've been hoping you *were* reading this right."

He smiled. "Good. I'm glad to hear it. I wasn't sure how you would react at first. Normally I'm not that impulsive, but you look gorgeous sitting here by the river. And that look in your eyes when you talked about trying to get my granddad and your neighbor back together—the timing seemed perfect."

"As long as we're in this together."

"Through thick and thin," he promised, taking her hand in his.

She prayed so. She couldn't take any more upheaval in her life right now.

twelve

Lance discovered that the antique center, the Country Shops of Culpepper, was holding a special open house the following weekend. When he called Connie with the news, they decided that this might prove their best opportunity to bring two people together in the hope of reconciliation. Connie sometimes wondered whether they were intruding after her encounter with Claudia Rowe. She only wanted peace in this situation. If there was one thing Connie desperately craved in her own life, it was peace. When she found out what life was like without it—that raw sense of anxiety mixed with an unsettled feeling like one lost in a dark forest—Connie did whatever was necessary to restore peace in her life. It was hard for her to understand how people like Claudia Rowe and Donna could live without the peace of God in their hearts. What did they do when the going got rough? Connie knew what Donna liked to do—shop or eat. Maybe Claudia was the same way with her antiques. Still she was hopeful that through all of this, God might open a door, not only to reconciliation but a hope in Him as well.

Connie eagerly prepared herself for the encounter with her neighbor. Before picking up the phone, she offered a prayer that the older woman would not shun her after what happened during their last visit. With the tears that were shed, along with the broken china, there seemed little reason to believe Claudia would agree to the excursion. She placed it all in God's hands.

Her confidence soared after making the call. Claudia was delighted to hear from her. Then came a surprise question— if Connie would come over and help her do some more packing.

"Since my daughters are so far away, there's no one here to help. And you did such a careful job the last time. I know we had that discussion about Gene, but that still doesn't mean you didn't do a wonderful job here. I'm grateful."

Connie smiled at this open invitation. She agreed to help, deciding to broach the subject about antique shopping after she arrived. There was little doubt that the best way to her neighbor's heart lay in offering a helping hand. Maybe if all went well, Connie would find her acquiescing to the excursion. Claudia would then run into Silas Westerfield, they would talk, and presto, love would be reborn like in the movies.

Connie arrived to find Claudia trying to pack heavy books into boxes. She scolded herself for not thinking of having Lance come help, especially with the heavier items. Two instead of one might have been helpful in this endeavor. Claudia greeted her with a pleasant smile, a glass of iced tea, and a request to help sort out some of the older books. They chatted about various topics until Connie mentioned Sally and the need to find her mother an antique rocking chair as a surprise birthday gift.

"Oh, rocking chairs," Claudia said with a sigh. "I have a book somewhere in this stack that shows many rocking chairs dating back several centuries. They were all made back then by superior craftsmen. It took precision work." She found a thick book on antiques and settled down on the sofa. "Yes, here it is. See how lovely they are?"

"Is it possible to find an antique like that in a store?"

"I'm not sure. Of course with the move and all, I haven't had a chance to look around at the antique stores here in town."

"Honestly, if I tried to look for one, I'd probably get something that was a fake. And I heard some good things about that antique center on Route 29. Any chance you might get some free time on Saturday to come with me and look at a few rocking chairs?"

A glint of anticipation danced in Claudia's eyes. "Oh, that would be lovely. I need to get out of this house. We can make an outing of it. We'll go antique shopping, and as my treat for all your help, I'll buy lunch."

Connie smiled smugly. This was going better than she had anticipated. And maybe after all was said and done, it would be Gene accompanying Bette to lunch. The mere thought sent tingles shooting straight down her spine. For all the concern over the outcome of this day, she could hardly wait to tell Lance how everything had fallen into place.

The afternoon flew by while they packed up the whole library. When she was ready to leave, Claudia thanked her profusely for her help. "I'm looking forward to antique browsing and lunch," Connie said. "Does ten thirty on Saturday sound good?"

"That's fine. See you Saturday."

Connie felt like she was floating on a cloud. She drifted down the sidewalk toward her apartment. Not only did she have the outing planned with Claudia Rowe, but the kisses of Lance Adams also lent energy to her steps. Nothing could be more perfect.

When she arrived home, she nearly embraced the cuckoo clock. The piece had been a trial at first, but doors were opening that had once been closed tight—like reconciliation, forgiveness, and for Connie, love. She wondered then what it would be like to be married to the assistant manager of a store. There was no sense in pondering that quite yet. Yes, Lance had kissed her, but there was still plenty of time before they would run down the aisle. At one time Connie vowed only to kiss the man she would marry. She had made that promise to herself long ago, even though she told no one about it—not even the few guys she had dated. When she opened herself up to accept Lance's kiss, she knew there was something special about him. And it wasn't just the kiss but his whole mannerism. They had been drawn together since day one and had only grown closer as time passed. Surely God would not have brought such a man into her life if he weren't meant to remain a permanent fixture in her heart.

Just then the phone rang. It was he, the man she thought of day and night.

"Hello, Connie."

He spoke her name in such a tender way that she nearly melted. The voice came from sweet lips that had touched hers just a few days ago. How she wanted to say, *Hello, Prince Charming. You have swept me off my feet,* but said simply, "Hi, Lance."

"So how did it go?"

"Marvelous! Absolutely marvelous. Claudia is definitely coming to the antique center this Saturday. And she plans to take me to lunch as a thank-you for helping her pack. I'm hoping it will turn into a luncheon date with you-know-who."

"Well, I hate to put a damper on all this, but there's a problem. Granddad refuses to go."

Her mouth fell open at this revelation. It never dawned on

her that Silas Westerfield wouldn't go. She was certain he wanted to see Claudia again but was too shy or proud to arrange such a meeting himself. "What? Why?"

"He knows this is all a setup. Granddad is pretty smart. Sure he might have been poor in money but definitely not in brains. He knows Bette will be there, and he knows what's going to happen—a tense scene he would rather not be a part of."

"How can he know what will happen? For all we know it could be a wonderful time for the both of them."

"You and I might believe that, but he doesn't. The mere idea makes him very nervous. It's been over forty years. A lot has changed, and he isn't a spring chicken anymore. He would rather do something less drastic, like call her on the phone maybe. But since she's moving, he feels it's all a waste of time anyway."

"But this is a perfect situation—in a nonthreatening setting that they both love. This is the time, Lance. It's now or never."

"For someone who wasn't sure about this whole thing, you're sure excited now."

"Of course I am. Claudia is anxious to go. I mean, I did give her the alibi about checking out rocking chairs, but it fit perfectly with our plan."

"I'm not sure what do from this end. I can't make Grand-dad go."

"Give me his phone number. Maybe I can try talking to him."

"You?"

"Why not? He did send me the beautiful basket of flowers. He knows I've been talking with my neighbor. To me that means there must be something there. If he was angry over my involvement, he would have sent a basket of poison ivy instead."

"Connie!"

"Well. . .the point is, maybe I have a little leverage. I did get the lowdown from Claudia about why they broke off their engagement. The least I can do is try."

Lance finally relented, giving her the phone number and telling her to call before 8:00 p.m. "But don't try to pull the wool over his eyes. He'll read right through it."

Connie promised. With the phone number in her hand, she thought about the words to say, as she had to do quite often these days. God again needed to guide the conversation. She did want to see things restored and prayed this message might be reflected in her words.

Later that evening, she dialed the number Lance had given her. When she introduced herself, she heard a cough.

"Miss Ortiz, this is a surprise."

Connie managed to clear the frog in her own throat. "Mr. Westerfield, I wanted to thank you for the lovely basket of flowers."

"You're quite welcome."

"I'm not sure I deserve it, but I wanted to thank you anyway."

"What? What do you mean you don't think you deserve it?"

"Oh, after the way I acted when you came calling. All I wanted to do was hold on to this cuckoo clock at all cost. I didn't even take into account your feelings."

She sensed his hesitancy. "But I know it was a priceless item that reminded you of your grandmother," he said.

"Yes, but you also mentioned how priceless it is to you as well. Of course I had no idea what you meant, but I know now. Love really is priceless when you think about it. We can own all the things in the world, even be rich as a king or sultan, but when it comes right down to it, love is the costliest possession of all."

Again, she felt his confusion on the phone. He coughed several times. "I'm not exactly sure why you're bringing this up."

"Well you see, I know your grandson quite well. And I've also been getting along with my neighbor, Mrs. Rowe."

"Really. In what way?"

"The Bible talks about the rewards one gets for being a servant. That's what I've been trying to do, not to put myself on a pedestal or anything. I've been helping her pack and all. I found out that sometimes it's the little acts of kindness that can win hearts. It's so easy to get caught up in our own little world. Once we break out of it to reach out to others, we find things we didn't even know existed. Companionship, conversation, even reconciliation. And these are all worth much more than any clock, don't you think?"

Silence came over the phone. Connie began to pray, hoping she hadn't overstepped her boundary. Sometimes her passion for a subject overshadowed discretion.

"I guess I've been trying to run away from it," he said slowly. "I'm a Christian, too, you see. I thought all I wanted was the clock, but what I really want is to reach out to the one who owned it. I'm afraid I'm too late."

"It's never too late, especially if God is in control. The only sure way to find out is to come to the antique center on Saturday with your grandson. God might surprise you."

He chuckled. "My dear girl, I've been surprised quite a bit by God and certainly not in ways I had anticipated. I had a wonderful marriage with my wife, Margaret, God bless her. I was content to live alone the rest of my life. But when I saw the ad for the yard sale at Bette's house and then saw she was selling our beloved clock, something stirred to life; something I thought was gone forever. At first I wanted to contact her. Then I thought perhaps if I got the clock, I could use it as a way to reach her."

"It's not too late, Mr. Westerfield. The best way to find out is to do a test this Saturday. I know that sometimes people abuse the Gideon-type test of hanging out fleeces, but it's okay to take a few steps forward and see where the path leads you. That's what I did, and that's how I found a clock and eventually your grandson."

"Lance has grown quite fond of you. He talks about you all the time. All right, I will consider it."

She sighed before hanging up the phone. It was all she could hope for, considering the circumstances. Now it was up to two wandering hearts and the Lord Himself to do the rest.

❧

Connie found her neighbor bubbling over with excitement as they drove through town to the antique center. Claudia shared about the town of Culpepper and how it had grown from when she was a little girl. She mentioned the store where Connie worked and how a large farm once stood there when she was a young girl. The owner happened to be a nice old man whose wife often baked cookies for church bake sales.

"I thought you only lived here a few years."

"I spent my childhood here. I moved away in my early twenties." She pointed to the rustic buildings that withstood the test of time. Those that used to stand were now replaced by modern shopping establishments and the solid brick buildings of downtown businesses. "I know towns change, but I wish some of the old places were still around. For instance, I remember the old soda shop. I was so sad when it closed two years ago. That's where my young man once bought me my first ice cream float. It was a wonderful time, too. Ice cream was cheap back then, certainly not like it is now. I once had to pay nearly three dollars for a simple hot fudge sundae with a cherry on top. I told the manager it was highway robbery. When I was growing up, such a treat would have cost thirty cents."

Connie nearly asked her if the young man she was referring to was Silas "Gene" Westerfield, but decided against it. She drove out onto the main highway and soon arrived at the antique center. The parking lot was overflowing with customers. Outside looked like a carnival. Vendors were selling homemade goodies and even cotton candy. Inside the center were all kinds of stately antiques from a bygone era. Connie was surprised to find items for sale that were available in recent memory—like older Barbie dolls, metal dollhouses, even an original little baking oven that outdated the newer models now available.

Claudia delved into the antiques as if she were young again, exclaiming over each one. She was a wealth of information, talking about the age of the item and its market value. Connie tagged along, trying to listen to her explanations, all the while wondering if Lance had arrived yet with his grandfather. When Claudia stopped to examine wares inside a curio cabinet, Connie spotted them across the aisle. She exhaled a sigh of relief. Lance caught her eye and nodded. Connie wondered how to proceed when Lance beckoned to her while his grandfather was engaged in a solid cherry bedstead. Connie told her neighbor she wanted to check out a booth across the way then slipped over to meet Lance at the end of the aisle.

"I'm so glad you're here," she whispered, giving him a hug of relief.

"I guess that talk you had with Granddad did the trick. I don't know what you said, but when I asked again if he would come, he said yes."

The two of them peered around a wooden pie safe to see Lance's grandfather making his way across the aisle. The man suddenly stopped short. Connie gasped, putting her hand on her chest to feel the rapid beating of her heart. This scene was almost too much to bear. Lance slipped his hand over hers and gave her a gentle squeeze of encouragement. They inched closer, hoping to hear bits and pieces of what was transpiring.

"I see you still like antiques," they heard Gene announce.

Bette whirled at the voice. She grabbed hold of the edge of the curio cabinet to steady her gait. "G—Gene!"

"Hello, Bette."

Bette bristled. A red flush filled her cheeks. "What are you doing here?"

"I suppose the same thing you're doing. Browsing."

Bette looked around hurriedly, as if scanning the establishment for Connie's whereabouts. Connie gripped Lance's hand as they ducked behind the pie safe. When they peered around it to observe the scene, Bette and Gene were staring at each other as if scrutinizing a memory from long ago.

"So how are you? I heard you're moving out of town."

"I'm fine," Bette said quickly, shoving the strap of her purse over her shoulder. "And yes, I am moving. The closing is a week from Monday. I'm moving to Virginia Beach to be with my daughters."

"That's nice." He gazed at the ground. "I knew you had

moved back here quite awhile ago, but I decided it wouldn't be wise to come calling."

"No, it wouldn't. We really have nothing to say to each other." She straightened then and folded her arms. "But I am curious to know why you were trying to hoodwink a young lady into selling you the cuckoo clock. When she told me how much you were willing to pay for it, I nearly had a coronary."

"It's really my business, Bette."

"No, it's mine. After all, it was my clock."

"It was *our* clock," he corrected. "I gave it to you on the condition of a promise."

"That was your promise, not mine. I never promised to marry you. It was your choice to give me some kind of fancy clock that I must say never saw the light of day."

The harsh words Claudia spoke were difficult to hear. Connie was surprised that Lance's grandfather didn't march away right then and there. She looked over at Lance, wondering how he felt about it all. Yet he only stood by as did his grandfather—two strong towers in the midst of a battle. His lips moved in silent prayer. Lance always knew the right thing to do in a difficult situation.

"I'm sorry to hear you say that," Gene continued. "It meant a lot to me, just as you do. I was hoping you might feel the same way."

"I'm sorry to say I don't. I suppose that now you've fallen by a little money with your antique dealing, you think I should fall all over you after forty years."

"Bette, you don't know me at all. I thought the love we once had would be able to see through the past. Yes, we did find love with others, and now have wonderful families because of it. But that doesn't mean we need to forget what we once had."

"Maybe you want to live in the past. I don't. It's gone. It's forgotten."

"Is it? The past has a way of influencing the future. I don't want the years I have left in this world clouded over by rumors that were never true. You must know it. Ask your heart, Bette. Maybe we can find somewhere to talk about it."

She shook her head and strode away. Connie bade Lance a hasty good-bye and headed toward a booth, just as Claudia approached. "I was just going to. . ." Connie began then paused. "Mrs. Rowe, is something wrong?"

Claudia took a tissue out of her purse and began blowing her nose. "I can't believe this happened. Right out of the blue, forty years later, he shows up wanting to reconcile."

"What do you mean?"

"Gene! I can't believe it. After all these years." She shook her head. "I'm sorry, but you'll have to take me home. I'm getting a terrible headache. He nearly made me have a nervous breakdown."

"What happened?"

She tearfully explained her encounter with Silas Westerfield while they headed for the car. "He's still the same man Daddy warned me about so many years ago. Serving his own self-interests. Trying to take over my life."

"Maybe he just wanted to say hello."

"Well, I know for a fact he wants that cuckoo clock. Just remember, you promised not to give it to him. I don't want him to have it. He'll parade it around like some kind of trophy, hoping I'll come running to him."

"And what if he does parade it around? What does the clock mean to him other than a representation of the love he once had for you?"

Claudia stared at Connie, speechless.

She started the car and headed for the road. "If I had someone who loved me that much, I would be so glad. I would thank God every day for it. That kind of love is hard to come by these days."

"H–he never really loved me. You didn't know him back then. He loved money and antiques."

"Maybe he did, but what he loves right now is the engraving of two names on the back panel of the cuckoo clock that speaks of something long ago. Yes, you both have suffered losses, but why not see if there's something else left while there's still time?"

Her face reddened. "I wish you would leave this situation alone. I appreciate your concern, but I need to deal with it as I see fit." She turned away and stared out the window. Connie could think of a million things she wanted to say but decided not to press the issue. She drove her neighbor home in silence. With a quick thank-you, Claudia got out of the car and strode away. Connie never felt lower in her life. All the joy she nursed over a possible reunion had evaporated into thin air. Now there was nothing but emptiness.

thirteen

After the episode at the antique center, Connie allowed the phone to ring in her apartment, even though she knew it was Lance. She felt confused by everything. Though the seed planting might have been admirable, the fruit from it was diseased. Connie always looked to the consequences of her actions. While she wanted things to come out right, when they didn't, she decided she must have done something wrong. If this were right, wouldn't God have blessed the encounter? Maybe the idea of setting up the meeting bordered on a deception that the Lord had frowned upon. At any rate, she felt miserable. Everything was hopeless.

Before church began on Sunday, Lance left his circle of friends to come find her. She had taken a seat in the back and began leafing through the Bible, hoping to lose herself within the pages. "Are you okay?" he asked. "I tried calling you, but there was no answer. I nearly went over to your place to knock on the door."

"I just wanted to be alone for a while."

"Did something happen between you and Mrs. Rowe?"

Connie shrugged.

Lance took a seat next to her, despite the looks they received from members of the congregation. Connie winced. No doubt everyone was eager to know if something was materializing between them. Why would it, after all? Lance was well thought of within the congregation. He served on many committees and was involved in helping lead the youth group. And he was the assistant manager of a megastore. She was just ordinary little Connie, a simple desk clerk, barely making ends meet.

"Hello, hello, wherever you are," Lance whispered in ear.

The sensation of his breath on her ear sent shivers racing up her spine. She nearly leaped to her feet. "Look, I just have a few things to think about." She stood then as the worship team came forward to lead the congregation in the opening song.

Lance left her to take his place with several men in a separate row. She sat alone in the row usually reserved for latecomers, trying hard to become a part of the worship. Yet self-pity clouded the time. She felt disillusioned about everything—Claudia Rowe, Silas Westerfield, her relationship with Lance, maybe even God.

When the service was over, Connie was quick to make a swift exit out of the church, but not as quickly as she'd hoped. Lance had left by a side entrance and was there at her car when she arrived.

"Well, aren't you Speedy Gonzales?" she murmured.

"I can see you're down in the dumps. Don't let yesterday bother you. I thought it was quite encouraging."

"Huh?" She stared at him in bewilderment.

"Sure. I mean you didn't think after forty-some years they would take each other in their arms and confess their love, did you? At least they're starting to talk about the past."

Connie fumbled for her keys. "I guess, if you call that progress."

"C'mon, I'll take you out for brunch. I know a little hole-in-the-wall that would be perfect. It's been around for ages. A locals' hangout called Baby Jim's. Granddad loves it."

"Baby Jim's, huh? Sounds like my kind of place." Connie reluctantly went along to his car. He said little as they drove to the old restaurant connected to the basement of a regular house. He led the way into the restaurant, filled to capacity with the after-church crowd. Customers were served every kind of greasy food available. Connie couldn't imagine this place being a hangout of Lance's grandfather's. She stood in line with Lance until he placed their order for two breakfast platters. Connie wasn't sure what to say but stared at the interior of the restaurant that represented the old-fashioned lunch counters of long ago. "I've passed this place a few times, but I've never been here."

"Like I said, this is the local hangout. It's been around since the thirties. They only serve breakfast and lunch. Granddad took me here a few times. He and Bette used to come here, too. We'll sit where they used to, at one of the picnic tables."

"Oh." Connie winced when he mentioned the sore subject of Gene and Bette. Of course they would end up sharing a meal at the same place where the couple once ate.

"What's on your mind?" he asked.

"I'm just trying to imagine Claudia Rowe and your grandfather as young people madly in love. Maybe they once sat there, side by side, sharing in a tall frosty milk shake and a plate of fries."

"For all I know, they did just that. They loved coming here. They also enjoyed strolls through the meadow that's now part of the park where we had our picnic."

Lance grabbed the platters while Connie took the drinks and headed for a picnic table. The eggs and sausage looked very appetizing, but right now the lump in Connie's throat quelled her hunger. Lance, on the other hand, dug right in.

She tentatively picked up the fork and took a few bites. It was good, despite the mood she was in. They said little else but enjoyed their brunch. Connie was glad for Lance's optimism, even after what they had witnessed at the antique center. She thought he might be deeper in the dumps than she was. She admired his faith in tough situations.

Finally, Connie put down her fork. "Maybe we should've never gotten involved, Lance. None of this is our business anyway."

"I beg to differ. It became our business when you bought the clock."

"Then I'll get rid of it. Maybe I'll give it to Donna. She can keep tabs on this whole situation. In fact, knowing her, she would probably love to be in the thick of things. I'll tell Claudia I gave it to a friend. I can't take much more of this."

Lance leaned over. His hand gently reached out to take up hers. She trembled under his touch. "Okay, what's this all about, Connie? You were so confident. Now you act like this is the worst thing that could have happened."

"I was just surprised at the hurt I saw between the two of them. Maybe I was expecting more, like words of kindness instead of bitterness. I know I couldn't expect a hug and kiss, but I thought after being separated over forty years they would be a little more friendly. Especially on my neighbor's part."

"Granddad was surprised by the encounter, I must admit. He said that Bette still has a lot of bitterness about the past. I tried talking to him, to make him see that maybe she doesn't really mean it, that she was just startled to see him. He believes she's still hounded by all that nonsense her father once planted in her brain. He had hoped all these years would make her see the light. He feels someone in that kind of darkness isn't worth pursuing."

"So it's hopeless."

"Connie, you and I both know that with God nothing is hopeless. These two had a falling out forty-some years ago. It was never resolved. This is why God wants us to reconcile with each other as soon as possible. It's a perfect example of what happens when too much time is allowed to elapse without a resolution. The heart can turn to stone."

"And it looks to me like they have no intention of resolving their differences. So what are we doing in the middle of it?"

Lance took his coffee and dumped in a cream and two packets of sugar. Instead of answering her question, he posed another. "Do you think we should give up?"

"I don't know. I've been considering it all night and most of the morning. Claudia has already told me to leave her alone. I don't have an invitation to communicate with her anytime soon. And she is set to move in a little over a week. I say we drop the whole thing."

"I think before we throw in the towel we should find out what to do. And I know just the ticket."

Connie was about to ask for details when she saw the twinkle in his eye. She realized they had been down this road before, with his wisdom shining like a bright bulb in a dark and difficult situation. "I know exactly what you're going to say. Pray and ask God."

"Bingo. I said you were sharp, and I meant it. Even if things don't go as planned, Connie, we need to persevere until God chooses to close the door. While Claudia may think she has closed the door, I'll wait for God to do it Himself. In the meantime, let's you and I both take the rest of this Sunday to take the matter to Him. I think it will surprise us to find out that He wants these two people to reconcile more than we do."

"I hope so. I don't want to think that the encounter inside the antique center has shut the door for good."

"This is a lot like the clock. I'll bet when you took it to the clockmaker, he probably did a little cleaning and all."

"He wanted to do more, but I didn't think it was necessary."

"Sometimes our hearts need a little fine-tuning and cleaning to make everything run in good order. I don't think anything here has been a mistake. God wants to use people, but they need a little sprucing up, even repairs to the damage in their lives. Once that's accomplished, I believe there's a destiny planned for Granddad and Mrs. Rowe, the same as I feel there's one for us."

The expectant look on his face told her that he might indeed be considering his own happiness as well as his grandfather's. It warmed her to think that he might think of her in that way. If only she felt as confident about the future.

He drove her back to church to pick up her car, rattling on about the days ahead and how God had everything planned out. After thanking him for brunch, she went home to ponder the encounter. Lance was indeed a rare gem. If only she didn't feel so doubtful about everything. Inside the apartment she barely heard the cuckoo singing until she glanced over at the tiny painted bird, making his appearance at the two o'clock hour. She came and took the clock off the wall. Putting it facedown on the table, she examined the engraving on the back. She thought of Lance's grandfather and his eagerness to buy the clock from her. If only there was some way to convince her neighbor that Silas Westerfield's intentions were genuine, that he still loved her even after all these years. But Claudia Rowe was a woman frozen to a belief that the man was only looking out for his own interests. It would be difficult to thaw out a heart like that and make her think otherwise.

Connie replaced the clock and decided to take a walk. It was a picture-perfect afternoon, with the sun gleaming and the temperature pleasant. She walked down the street until she came to Claudia Rowe's house. It sat still and quiet. Most of the boxes on the porch were gone. The storage shed was open, revealing the boxes stacked inside, ready for the moving van when it appeared. She swallowed hard. If Claudia moved away before reconciliation could take place, it would spell the end for the couple's chances. They would go their separate ways and never look back.

Connie continued on, dreaming of walking down the aisle into Lance's arms. Flowers surrounded the pebbled path. The breeze sent her fine veil billowing. She could see a perfect church set up in God's glory, beneath the trees at the park where she and Lance first shared in a kiss. A true covenant would commence in that special place. If only there was some way for another couple by the name of Gene and Bette to likewise make such a commitment.

Connie returned home, anxious to call Lance and tell him about her dream—just the part about Gene and Bette. He'd talked about them having a future, but she knew it would be presumptuous of her to tell him she'd been daydreaming about walking down the aisle into his arms.

When he answered, she said, "Hi, Lance. I've got another idea. Maybe we should set up a table for two in that special grove of trees by the river, the same place where we had our talk. We can tell your grandfather and my neighbor there will be a picnic, but instead, it will be a private get-together."

"Are you serious? Why the sudden change?"

"I was thinking about weddings and saw a beautiful one in God's creation, right there in the park. I think it would be nice if your grandfather and Claudia could meet one final time. In a place like that, anything can happen: Look at us."

"Weddings, huh?" Lance chuckled softly. "It's a nice idea, except I don't believe they would fall for another outing. What's the saying? Fool me once, shame on you; fool me twice, shame on me."

"I don't think Claudia suspects that I set her up at the antique center. Your grandfather knew about the encounter, but she didn't. So it wouldn't seem out of the ordinary to have a picnic in the park, at least from her point of view."

"I thought Mrs. Rowe asked you not to be involved anymore."

"She did. I'm thinking perhaps of trying to get one of her daughters or a friend to help out. Someone she knows who might be willing to invite her to a gathering."

"I'm not sure, Connie. If you ask and the daughter doesn't want her mother involved, it could boomerang. We know from Bette's past that having family caught up in everything isn't always the best solution."

"Good point. Then what would you suggest? I'm out of ideas."

There was such a long pause Connie thought the call had terminated.

"Lance?"

"I'm still here. Just thinking about what you said and how we can get them both to the park for a picnic. I still don't think it would be wise to involve her family. Maybe if we pretend to have a gathering hosted by friends—like a going-away celebration since she's moving away. That might work."

"What about your grandfather? How would you get him to come to the park?"

"Oh, Granddad likes a stroll in the park anytime, so long as we take it easy. I'll pack us a lunch, and he'll think we're going there for our own picnic and to talk about business. He likes it when I ask him for advice. He's always giving me pointers from a business standpoint."

"Maybe I can find out about the friends Claudia has in the area. If she thinks it's a friendly get-together to see her off, she wouldn't be suspicious. Since she's moving, especially as far away as Virginia Beach, it would make sense that people would want to give her a send-off."

"Sounds like you have a plan, lady. Let me know if I can help in any way."

☙

Connie immediately went to work creating an invitation on the computer. She paused to consider it all, realizing the whole thing could fall apart if Claudia refused to come. She dare not deliver the invitation herself after the fiasco at the antique center. She considered the neighbors in the area who might help and recalled the elderly couple living next door to Claudia. Perhaps they would be helpful in encouraging her to accept the invitation.

Connie spruced up her hair, grabbed her purse and the invitation, then made her way down the street. She carefully sneaked up to the neighbor's house, hoping Claudia wouldn't suddenly glance out her window and catch her moseying up the driveway.

At the door, a kindly woman answered. "Hello. I think I recognize you."

"I'm Connie Ortiz. I live down the street in the apartment building."

"Yes, that's right. I'm Hilda McCall. Would you like to come in?"

Connie was grateful for the open invitation. She went in and, to her astonishment, saw a cuckoo clock hanging on the wall. She nearly gasped out loud but managed to control her emotions. "I'm sorry for barging in like this," she began.

"It's no bother. I was just telling Stanley the other day that we really don't know many of our neighbors except for Claudia. And now she's moving away. The last I heard, some young couple bought her house."

"Do you know Mrs. Rowe very well?"

"Oh yes, ever since she moved in. She has so many beautiful antiques. We get together for coffee sometimes."

"I actually bought one of her antiques at the yard sale she had not too long ago. Would you believe it was a cuckoo clock?"

"Really?" Hilda's gaze settled on her own clock hanging on the wall. "Aren't they just precious?"

"Yes, and it just so happens that the clock was involved in a mystery of sorts." Connie delved into the history of the clock and how it symbolized the love between Claudia and Lance's grandfather named Gene. Hilda listened with interest.

"You know, I seem to recall Claudia mentioning a certain gentleman in her past. She said she nearly married him but they had a falling out."

"Well, believe it or not, Gene's grandson, Lance, and I are hoping there might be some sparks left. They both have been widowed for many years. I know that Gene really wants to talk to her. But Mrs. Rowe hasn't been too keen on the idea.

So Lance and I came up with a plan, a picnic for two at the park. The problem is, I don't think Mrs. Rowe will go if she knows Gene will be there. So I was thinking of having someone invite her to a pretend farewell party given by her friends. I immediately thought of you, since you are her closest neighbor."

"Will this Gene be at the party?"

"That's the point. The party will not be a true party at all but a special picnic for the two of them. Lance and I want to see them come together if possible and try to work out their differences."

"So the party idea is a ruse for a special picnic. You're going to an awful lot of trouble, Connie. Why are you doing this, if I might ask?"

Connie paused. Why did she want to do this? "I've never really considered it up until now. I have no personal reasons for bringing them together, I guess. But Gene is Lance's grandfather. And they are very close. If his grandfather's happiness means Lance's happiness, then I'll do what I can to see it through."

Hilda laughed. "Aha, I see. But you must know if Claudia doesn't want to associate with the man, then there's nothing you can do to make it happen. Even if your intentions are good."

"Oh, I understand. But I don't see any harm in trying one more time for a reunion between the two of them before she leaves this area for good. It might mend both their hearts instead of having them hurt for the rest of their lives. And I've talked with Mrs. Rowe about the past. Believe me, I can tell she's hurting. Sometimes talking things out is the best medicine in the world."

"I can't argue with that. Stanley and I have talked through many difficulties, even when it was uncomfortable."

Connie withdrew the envelope. "This is the invitation. I was wondering if you might take this over to Claudia and see if she will come. I thought since you knew her, she might agree to it."

Hilda stared first at the envelope then at Connie. "I don't know what it is that makes you young people get involved in things like this. I hope it's worth the effort."

"It will be if two broken hearts are mended."

Hilda smiled as she took the envelope. "I'll take it over to Claudia and let you know what she says. And I do know a few friends of hers. I can have them call and encourage her to come."

"That would be wonderful. Thank you so much." Connie nearly danced her way down the sidewalk. At least she had put the wheels in motion. Now it was up to the Lord to make it everything work out to the final destination, wherever it ended up.

fourteen

So far the plan had worked, according to Hilda McCall who had phoned Connie with Claudia's reaction to the invitation.

"At first Claudia was startled to think anyone would care enough to throw her a going-away bash. She went on to say she hoped there wouldn't be too many people, as she didn't like crowds." Hilda chuckled. "You know, I actually enjoyed being a part of this secret," she confessed. "In a way I wish I was throwing the surprise party."

"If all goes well, maybe you can throw an engagement party instead."

Connie could just picture Hilda on the other end, shaking her head in wonder. "Don't you beat all, young lady. I've never seen anyone so determined. I guess if it's meant to be, it will happen. But if it's not, then you must be willing to let it go. You can't force two people to reconcile, no matter how much you may want it to happen. Ultimately it's between them and the Lord."

Connie agreed. How often she wanted to change the circumstances of life through her own devices. She prayed she wouldn't suffer disappointment if things didn't go the way she planned. One might sow the seed and another might water it, but only God can cause the growth.

During the rest of the week, Connie was on the phone with Lance, sometimes several times a night, to go over details concerning the picnic. He'd marveled at her ingenuity, especially at recruiting the neighbors to help with the whole scheme.

Near the end of the week, they met at her place to finalize the menu that would be served up on china plates. As they discussed it, Connie thought about the two of them. How like Bette and Gene they were, two young people in love, but one well-off and the other poor. What would she do if Lance's family suddenly decided to treat her as an outcast? What if they convinced Lance to abandon her as Bette did to Gene? How would she ever live through that kind of rejection?

"You've gotten quiet all of a sudden," Lance remarked, staring at her in confusion. "Is something the matter with these plans?"

Connie traced her finger across a pillow decorating the old sofa that once belonged to her grandmother. "Just thinking about something."

"Thinking can sometimes cause more harm than good, Connie. And just to make sure it comes out right in the end, I'll offer a twenty-dollar bill instead of a penny for your thoughts."

She wanted to giggle at his play on words that spoke of his affection, but somehow the offer of money made her feel worse. He could put down twenty dollars if he wanted. She was lucky if she could put down a dime. Her finances certainly hadn't worsened as they had when she purchased the clock, but they hadn't improved much either. There were still weeks of penny-pinching no matter how much she scrimped and saved.

Lance reached into his pocket, took out his wallet, and withdrew a twenty-dollar bill. "Here. Take it. I'm desperate to find out what's happening in that pretty head of yours."

"I don't want your money. I just want to make sure there aren't any bombshells coming our way."

"Like what?"

She hesitated. He would think her foolish if she came out with it. But the consequences could be far worse if she stayed silent. It would be better to settle things now before they went any deeper with their relationship. "I need to know something. Are your parents against you being with someone who isn't financially secure?"

His eyebrows lowered in confusion. "What brought this up?"

"We're trying to bring together two people who split apart because of finances. One of the families did everything in their power to break up the engagement. I don't want that happening to us. So if there's any chance at all, then maybe it would be better for us to go our separate ways now and not get hurt."

"Connie, you're not making any sense. You know my job is secure."

"Not yours," she said in exasperation. "Mine. I'm the one as poor as a mouse. I was hardly able to buy groceries last month. I don't want your parents unhappy because you're hooked up with someone so poor."

To her dismay, Lance bit his lip as if to stifle a chuckle. "Do you honestly think that will happen?"

"I don't know. Can it?"

"Connie, if you must know, I'm the first one in my family to get a managerial position. Everyone has to save to make ends meet, except perhaps for my sister, Alice. She's making a heap of money right now, but she worked hard like all of us to get where she's at. I've learned valuable lessons, too—that one's walk with God and their loved ones are far more important than how many bucks a person makes. Granddad learned that, also. And I'm hoping Bette will see the light and realize that what her father did to their relationship long ago was foolish.

Sure we need money to exist, but there are other things more important."

"So I won't get looked down on by someone better off, like your sister?" Connie cringed at the thought of this Alice calling her up, asking her how much money she made before pronouncing her a leech to the entire Adams clan. In turn, they might shun her as Bette's family did to his grandfather. She would be left with nothing but the memory of a love gone sour and the monotony of a job behind a customer service counter.

"In case you didn't know it, you already have a fan club. Granddad has been telling everyone what a wonderful lady you are. All my sisters want to meet you. They think you'd be perfect for someone like me." He chuckled. "They all want to help plan a huge wedding."

Connie grinned at the thought. It would be nice to have sisters to talk to. And her brother Louis would enjoy getting to know Lance. Maybe Lance could even influence Henry's life, too. Only God's divine hand could bring it to pass.

"So have I put your worries to rest?" he asked.

"I guess so."

"I will admit, though, that your questions have confirmed some things that God has been speaking to me about."

"Like what?"

"I'll let you know as time goes by. But for now let's put the finishing touches on this picnic for two."

Connie went over the menu once more, yet now she was clearly distracted by his comment. What could God have been whispering to him in that still, small voice? Just when she had one question answered, another came to take its place. There was little time to ponder it while planning out the final details for the reunion between Bette and Gene.

At work the next day, Connie took out a notepad and began jotting down what they would need for the outing. *Small table* went on the list. *Pure white tablecloth and candlesticks in pewter holders.* The menu of chicken cordon bleu sounded elegant to Connie, accompanied by a bottle of sparkling cider served up in crystal goblets. She was furiously writing when a face peered over her shoulder, examining the paper.

"Wow, is all that for our manager?" Donna inquired with a smirk.

Connie covered the paper with her hand. "It's a secret."

"Oh, Connie, don't keep secrets from me. Are you planning a special dinner?"

"Yes, but it's not who you think. It's for Lance's grandfather and the lady he once loved."

"Oh, how sweet." Donna gently pushed Connie's hand away from the paper. "Sounds nice. Where do you plan on having it?"

"At the park. We found a really nice place. And I managed to get Bette's neighbor in on it. She's invited Bette to the park under the guise that some friends are throwing her a farewell party. Actually, it will be an intimate dinner with Gene, though Bette doesn't know it yet."

Donna's eyes sparkled at the romantic ploy about to unfold. "I never knew you had it in you, Connie. I mean you do know how to plan get-togethers, but it's amazing to see what you're doing for these people in particular. They've become your special project."

"I had a good trainer." When Donna raised an eyebrow, Connie pointed the pen at her. "Who was the one who first pointed out Lance to me? Who kept insisting I sell the clock, which eventually led to Claudia making a surprise visit at my apartment? And who discovered the mystery of the clock by going with me to the clock shop and finding that engraving on the back panel?"

Donna giggled and sat down beside to Connie. "I thought at first you considered me a bit too opinionated for my own good. I never told you this, but my parents always put me down for everything I did. I had an older sister who went into modeling, and they thought she was the greatest. I felt like I always had to compete with her. They would ask me why I couldn't do something with my life. When I left the house, I decided I would make something of myself. Of course I didn't think that this store would be a stopover along the way. I hope one day to go back to school and maybe work on a business degree. I wouldn't mind doing what Lance is doing—being a manager and all. I like working with people."

"I'll tell him."

Donna grabbed her arm. "Oh, don't tell him that! I don't have a degree anyway."

"But maybe he has some ideas on how you can further your career so you can become what you want to be. I really believe we have God-given goals for our lives. Like you, I'm wondering how this job will fit into my future plans. But I know if I didn't work here, I wouldn't have met you or Lance or had my adventure with a famous cuckoo clock." She chuckled at the wonder of it all. "Yet here I am. God worked it out for Lance to become a part of my life. And I think real soon he may even ask me to marry him."

"Wow. So it's heading in that direction already?"

Connie couldn't help blushing. "It seems that way. His family wants to plan the wedding. As nurses sometimes fall in love with their patients, it seems a manager may have fallen in love with his employee."

"How sweet." Donna fumbled with several register receipts

she held in her hand. "So you really think God is running your life, don't you?"

"I know He is. I wouldn't have made it this far if He wasn't. It's much better having someone else at the helm. I'd probably mess it all up; maybe even end up like my brother Henry who's still searching for his identity. But I'm glad I found my identity in God. I'd much rather have His plans for my life than any other."

Donna didn't reply but went over to the register where a line of customers had begun forming. Connie didn't realize the store had opened for business. She was so intent on sharing her love for the Lord that the time had flown by. But she sensed a joy in her heart concerning Donna. Even if she wasn't the one to bring her friend to the Lord, at least she could throw down a seed now and then.

❧

The day of the picnic arrived. Connie was more nervous than she had ever been in her life. She wondered what led her to do strange things like this. It must be that special Someone who had given her the grace to go forth. Most people would let life run its course and not get involved. But she was heavily involved now. Her neighbor was once the love of Lance's grandfather. All of them had been united by her cuckoo clock. She felt obligated to at least try to make something wonderful happen.

She gingerly placed a box containing dinnerware in the backseat of the car. Lance arranged for a waiter from a nearby catering business to arrive at the appointed time and serve the couple dinner. Lance had taken care of the music—supplied by his portable CD player—and the small table and chairs. The night before, while they finalized plans on the phone, Connie could hear the excitement radiating in his voice. She sensed his hope regarding his grandfather and her neighbor. If the Lord meant it to be, everything would work out.

Connie asked if Hilda and her husband could bring Claudia to the event in the park. At first Hilda balked at the idea. After seeing the energy and enthusiasm put into the meeting, Hilda agreed it was the best thing to ensure that Claudia arrived as planned.

Connie drove over to the park and headed for the grove of trees to find Lance setting up the table and chairs. He also brought along a few other chairs as well.

"What are those for?" she inquired.

"I don't want your neighbor thinking this is a setup. Some extra chairs around will convince her at first that this is an actual party. He then put up a small stepladder, and with Connie's help, looped streamers through the tree branches.

"I didn't know you had a decorator's touch, Mr. Adams," she teased.

"I didn't know I had a knack for devious undertakings either." He glanced at his watch. "I'll need to pick up Grand-dad soon. I promised him that innocent walk, you know." He gave her a wink as he reached the bottom of the ladder. He drew Connie into his arms. "How about a kiss and a prayer for God's grace on this event?"

Connie accepted his kiss with enthusiasm. They then clasped hands and prayed for God's will to be done. When Lance left, Connie suddenly felt lonely and anxious. She gazed into the trees and at the streamers fluttering in the gentle breeze. A chill suddenly overcame her. What if this didn't work? What if all this planning was for naught? She refused to allow doubt to creep in at this important moment. She wouldn't be like the ocean waves rolling in and out, going nowhere as the Bible talked about in the book of James. She believed God would perform a miracle here in this grove by the river, if not for Gene and Bette, then for her and Lance.

Time slowly ticked by. When the hour drew near, Connie took her place behind some nearby bushes to await the gathering. Five minutes passed. Ten. Twenty. She saw Lance and his granddad moseying up the paved walkway. Panic assailed her. Claudia and Hilda were nowhere in sight. Where were they? Had something happened? She saw Lance pause with his granddad, talking about something, yet she could clearly see the worried look on his face.

"Looks like someone is having a party here," Silas Westerfield noted.

"It sure does." Lance glanced at the bushes toward Connie. When his granddad wasn't looking, he mouthed the words, *Where is Bette?*

Connie shrugged her shoulders and pointed to her watch, telling him they were late.

Forty-five minutes had elapsed. Lance and his granddad had already moved along with their walk. Connie felt she might faint. Her limbs began to tremble. The emotion of it all was too great. All their plans, all that seeking, everything had fizzled out before it began. She wanted to break down and cry. Instead, she shoved the strap of her purse over her shoulder and made for the trees, ready to take everything down.

Suddenly she heard voices in the distance.

"Why, it does look like a party," Claudia was saying. Connie darted behind the bushes. Her heart thumped wildly. She saw Hilda guiding Claudia over to the grove.

"We wanted to make sure you had a proper send-off," Hilda said. "So we had lunch catered. Today you will be served like a queen." Hilda pulled out a chair at the small table for Claudia to sit.

Connie wanted to cry. Hilda was doing such a splendid job with all this. Now if only Lance would return with his grand-dad. At last she saw them heading back down the paved path that led through the park. Lance backpedaled and disappeared. Hilda, as well, took her husband by the arm and walked off, telling Claudia they were going to find the caterer.

"Wait a minute!" Claudia exclaimed, standing to her feet. She turned, and to her shock, saw Gene approaching the outdoor dining area. "What's going on? I thought this was supposed to be a going-away party given by friends."

He looked around. "I guess all these friends had other plans."

She began to shake. "This was all a setup, wasn't it? I don't believe it."

"I do. Don't you see what's going on here, Bette? There are people who really love us. They want us to take time to be alone."

"I was deceived." She began to walk away in a huff.

"Yes, you have been deceived for a very long time. Forty years to be exact. Maybe it's about time you tasted a bit of the truth." Gene limped over and took a seat. To his apparent surprise, Bette sudeenly turned around and sat down opposite him. She kept her gaze focused on her lap.

"I don't believe they did this," she murmured. "And Hilda, of all people. Why?"

She looked up, and her jaw dropped when a waiter and an assistant appeared in the grove, carrying silver dishes full of food. Lance's granddad pulled a handkerchief from his pocket to wipe his eyes and blow his nose.

"Look at this," his voice choked out as the table was arranged. The waiter poured out goblets of sparkling cider. Slowly Gene lifted his glass. "Bette, even if our paths take us in opposite directions, I'm glad we can at least enjoy the love that others have for us together. It will be a fond memory."

Bette's hand shook as she raised her glass to her lips. She took one tiny sip, then set it down. "I don't think I can go through with this."

Gene lifted a silver cover off the platter to reveal the steaming chicken cordon bleu, wild rice, and asparagus encircled with red pimento. "You mean you can't enjoy this wonderful meal? Look at the love, not to mention the money and effort that went into this. Even if you say nothing more to me the rest of the meal, we can pretend to enjoy it and be gracious toward those who thought enough of us to do such a wonderful thing."

Lance curled his arm around Connie, watching from their place behind the bushes as Bette and Gene began to eat. Perhaps for the first time in forty years they would actually share pleasant conversation over a meal together. What she saw and heard filled her with expectation.

The couple continued to eat the lunch. At one point Connie saw her neighbor lift her head and laugh. She squeezed Lance's hand. It seemed almost unbelievable to see this happening after the events they had witnessed at the antique center.

Just then Lance took her by the hand and propelled her away.

"What are you doing?" she whispered. "Don't you want to see what's happening?"

"I've seen plenty to know that they need to be alone, and I mean really alone. They've both been through a lot. Only God can make right what's happened between them."

"But. . ." Connie stared back at the grove of trees and the streamers waving as if to say farewell. The mere idea that she couldn't see the end results of their handiwork left her with a nagging feeling inside. Now she would have to wait for the results, and for how long she didn't know.

"Besides, I thought maybe you would like to go on a walk with me." When she didn't say anything, he tugged on her hand. "Connie?"

"Of course I want to take a walk with you. But maybe they could use. . ."

"Our help?" He laughed. "I think we've done enough. Sometimes you have to let go and allow people to find their own course in life. If you try to do it all on your own, you can get hurt if things don't work out the way you planned."

"I know. I've been there, many times." When she did let go and allowed God to work, events happened that she couldn't begin to explain. Then she knew it came from His hand and no one else's.

The soft breeze felt wonderful on her face after all the stress of the last few hours. What felt even more wonderful was the presence of Lance at her side. They stopped at a pic-nic table. Nearby on a patch of sandy ground, a furious game of volleyball was in progress.

"Have you ever played?" he asked.

"I'm terrible at it."

"Let's see." He grabbed her hand and led her forward.

"Lance, what are you doing?"

He didn't answer but asked the team leaders if they could to join in. Connie found herself and Lance on opposing teams. *This is all I need, another embarrassing moment in my life.* Why was he making her do this? Thankfully, the ball rarely came to her. Instead, she watched Lance's athletic abilities as he dove for the ball, including several spikes that sent cheers rippling through his team. When it came time for Connie to serve, she looked at the ball with uncertainty. Lance stood near the net, a smile on his face and waving at her to serve the ball to him.

She served, sending the ball sailing over the net between two players.

"Hey, good serve!" said a guy next to her.

Connie's confidence rose. She served another ball, which Lance dived to intercept. Instead he fell flat on his face. Sand covered his fine trousers and polo shirt. Yet he looked as if he were having the time of his life. After several more serves, Connie decided to call it quits. Her wrist stung from the smack of the ball. Lance thanked the teams for allowing them to play and escorted her back to the picnic table.

"Was that fun or what?"

"Or what," she pronounced, massaging her reddened arm.

He took up her arm and kissed the tender area. "I hope you don't mind that we played. I used to love volleyball as a kid. Sometimes when the going gets rough, it's good to be a kid again."

"I'm learning more about you every day, Lance Adams. Especially the man who doesn't mind getting rough and tough in his nice clothes."

"I hope you'll want to know even more. And I want to know everything about you, too." He took her hand and held it in his.

Connie inhaled a short breath. It seemed their relationship was growing more serious by the moment. Yet the mere notion that a marriage proposal might be looming on the horizon made her shudder. Was she ready for it?

fifteen

Connie waited patiently for some word as to how the picnic in the park finally ended. When she called Lance for the news, he only said his grandfather told him little about the event. "We're just going to have to be patient."

Connie sighed. How she hated waiting. If the picnic didn't unite the two of them, nothing would, in her humble opinion. She took the matter to prayer, entrusting it to God as she prepared for a day of yard sales. Donna had agreed to tag along with her. That morning she had rushed out to buy the paper, and to her delight, found a place that was selling a used rocking chair. When Donna arrived, she immediately told her they were on a scouting expedition for the chair.

"I have my list, also," Donna said. "Lamps, some glasses, Avon cosmetics, red pumps—"

"Wow. Do you really think you're going to find all that?"

"Honey, with you I never know what's going to happen!"

Connie smiled and grabbed her purse. They drove down the road, slowly past her neighbor's house that now appeared dark and dismal since the sale closing had finalized. In another few weeks a young couple would be moving in. If only she knew what had transpired between her neighbor and Lance's grandfather.

As if reading her mind, Donna asked, "Have you heard the results of your little dinner escapade at the park?"

Connie shook her head. "Nothing. The picnic went well, I

thought, but Lance says his grandfather has been tight-lipped about it all. To me, that must mean bad news."

"You can lead a horse to water, but you can't make him drink. At least everything is on track between you and Lance, right?"

Connie became silent at that point. Donna cast her a look. "Don't tell me you two had an argument."

"No, no. It's just that I think Lance is ready for the fast track, and I'm still trying to find my way through the jungle."

"I thought you were the one who said marriage was on the horizon, and you were ready to accept it with open arms."

"Donna, it didn't seem real back then. It was more like a fairy tale. Now that it might be happening, I'm scared to death."

Donna patted her arm. "You have nothing to fear. This is a great guy you've snagged. I knew it from the get-go. Besides, you're the one telling me that we should be trusting God with our lives."

"You're right. If this wasn't in God's big plan, He wouldn't let me go through with it."

Donna said little else as they continued the drive out to the country and a large home with many wares spread out on tables. At once, Connie made for the rocking chair. It was nice piece, similar in style to the ones she had seen in Claudia's book on antiques. When she asked the price, it seemed a little steep. But Sally had said to pay whatever price, especially if the piece was in excellent condition.

Once more, Connie handed over all the money in her wallet, including some of her own cash as well as the money Sally had given her. She knew Sally would pay back the difference. Donna also found several items, among them a pair of red high heels.

"This is great," Connie exclaimed when they returned to the car, lugging the chair. They heaved it into the trunk then tied down the back hatch with a piece of rope. "Success at last! Honestly, after the episode with the clock, I never thought I would go to another yard sale."

"Yeah, you and that clock of yours. What a tale you have to tell."

Connie had to admit it was an interesting twist in her life, bringing with it the blessing of Lance Adams. Pondering it all and the way she and Lance worked together to unite two long-lost loved ones eased her misgivings about a future commitment. It didn't matter to Lance that she worked under him at the department store with a salary that barely covered the monthly bills. What mattered to him was the love in their hearts, placed there by God Himself.

Connie arrived back at her apartment with the rocking chair, only to find a strangely familiar car parked out in front of her apartment. She gazed back at Donna thinking, *Not again!* Inside the vehicle were two passengers. One of them slowly came out of the car, dressed in a purple pantsuit and a pearl necklace that glimmered in the sunlight. It was Claudia Rowe, alias Bette.

She waved at Connie, her face one huge smile. Connie stared so hard she thought her eyes would go dry.

"Is that who I think it is in the driver's seat?" Donna asked.

Sure enough it was Silas "Gene" Westerfield, decked out in a black suit. He waved as well but remained behind the wheel of the car. Connie didn't know he owned a car; then she recognized the vehicle as the one that had sat for ages in Claudia's driveway.

"I hope you don't mind this intrusion," Claudia said. "I just had to see you."

"Of course. Come on in." They stepped inside the house, just as the cuckoo had finished a round of chirping. "This is my friend, Donna. Donna, my neighbor, Mrs. Rowe."

Donna politely shook her hand.

"Again, I hope you don't mind me stopping in," Claudia began. "Gene and I are on our way to Fredericksburg. There are some fine antique shops there, you know. And he's taking me out to dinner afterward."

Connie wanted to shout *Hallelujah!* when she heard this news. Instead, she said, "I'm so glad, Mrs. Rowe."

"I. . .well, we also wanted to thank you for caring about us so much. I honestly thought you were a strange young woman with strange ideas. Maybe even a busybody. But I'm so glad you were. I'm still in shock." A lone tear drifted down her cheek. Connie handed her the tissue box, which she took with a smile as if remembering their first visit. "I once thought my children were the only ones who cared about me. It took all of this to realize what love is really all about. You and that young man of yours had the heart to bring together two old people who might have lost something very special."

"Connie knows how to do everything up big," Donna added.

"Yes, she does and more. Without her, I wouldn't have understood the terrible mistakes I had made. And why Gene decided to come back to me after all this, it simply amazes me. I guess that's love, right?" She wiped her tears away with a tissue. "I must admit, one of the best things that ever happened to me was your coming to my yard sale that Saturday and buying the cuckoo clock. If I had buried it away or even thrown it out, I would have thrown away the best opportunity to experience love again."

Connie reached out and gave her a brief hug. "I'm so happy for you."

Claudia blew her nose. "Anyway, I just had to tell you this personally. Gene is waiting for me, so I need to go."

"Wait a minute, please." Connie gazed at the cuckoo clock that had accomplished yet another miracle. Slowly she took it down from its place on her wall. "You forgot something. I believe this is yours."

"Oh no. You keep it."

"Mrs. Rowe, it's not my name on the back. I can look for another one. As I recall, a handsome man once gave you this clock and with the most romantic words I've ever heard. 'As time endures, so will our love.'"

Claudia again blew her nose. "Yes, he did say that. All right, I will accept it. At least we can pay you for it."

"No, that's fine. You both have paid me more than the clock is worth and then some." Connie went to the back room to retrieve the dusty box and carefully packed up the timepiece. "So long, Mr. Cuckoo. You're going home."

Claudia bid her farewell with the box tucked under her arm. Connie peeked out between the blinds as Claudia entered the car and promptly showed the clock to Gene. He rolled down the window, and to Connie's surprise, gave her a thumbs-up signal.

"Can you believe that?" Connie said with a laugh. "Isn't it amazing?"

Donna watched the car speed away. "All of this is unbelievable," she murmured.

"You think so?"

"This whole saga. I know I gave you encouragement and ideas about getting those two back together, but honestly I had no idea it would really work. And there they are, taking off like two lovebirds. It's unreal."

"Miracles can happen, Donna, especially when God is in control."

Donna fingered the lace curtain adorning the window. "Hey, Connie, would it be okay if I try out your church tomorrow?"

"That would be great, Donna! I'd love to have you come along. Did you know it's the same church Lance goes to?"

"I'm really interested in what's happened here. I'll have to admit, I wouldn't mind a miracle or two in my life. Just seeing this all play out, especially how you and Lance were determined to make things work, has got me thinking. I never went to church much. My family didn't practice religion except on holidays. If God was around, He was just a building with a steeple on top. But you live like He's real, standing right there beside you."

"It's hard to understand, Donna, but it's true. He's closer than any friend. He cares so much about each of us. He knows what's best for us, even if we don't know ourselves. Tell you what—Lance and I will pick you up, then we'll catch brunch at our newest hangout. It's this wild place that Lance introduced me to not too long ago. They make a great breakfast, be it a little greasy."

"Okay." She offered a hesitant smile before picking up her yard sale purchases. "See you later."

Connie felt a rush of the warm fuzzies after what she had witnessed this day. It began with finding the rocking chair, then the miraculous encounter with Claudia Rowe, only to end with Donna interested in attending church. Now there remained but one puzzle piece left to complete the picture of blessing.

&

Sunday came. Donna appeared to enjoy the service immensely. Connie was glad to see her enthusiasm. She would have rejoiced more were it not for Lance's unexplained absence. She decided he must either be sick or involved in something important. She tried calling him at home but received no answer. He had never let her go more than a day or two without some method of communication, whether at work or by phone. Connie ended up taking Donna to Baby Jim's by herself, then spent the rest of the day at the apartment wondering what was going on.

The next morning, Connie anticipated seeing Lance at the store. She made up her mind to be friendly to him, even if he did leave her in the dark about his absence over the weekend. To her disappointment, he never appeared. When she moseyed on back to the office to check on him, the secretary said he was away on business. Connie thought it odd that he would go on a trip without telling her. On her lunch break, she tried numerous times to reach him on his cell phone, but his voice mail was full. There was still no response at home either.

When several more days trickled by without a word from him, Connie finally decided to give his grandfather a call. It was the only thing left to do.

"All I know is that he said he would be out of town, Miss Ortiz."

"He didn't leave a message or anything about what he's doing?"

"He did say he would be seeing the family. I'm sure he will

call you when he gets back."

Connie hung up the phone, more confused than ever. It just didn't seem like Lance to take off without saying anything. Suddenly fear hit her broadside like a car smashing into a brick wall. What if his family had talked him out of associating with her? Just like Silas Westerfield, when Claudia's family turned her against him and they were forever shut out of each other's lives. Connie began biting her nails, something she hadn't done since she was a teenager. Maybe one of his sisters had run a check on her and found out how poor she was. Maybe they didn't like the idea of him associating with someone who had a Hispanic background. Now it had come down to this.

She began to pace, looking up at the empty wall space where the cuckoo clock once hung. There was nothing to fill the void, nothing but the awful image of Lance sending her a letter informing her this wasn't going to work between them, that his family had said no, or he had found a wealthy woman who was the manager of a sister store. Oh, why hadn't she been truthful about her feelings at the onset? She should have come right out and told him she loved him, that she wanted to spend the rest of her life with him no matter how much money they earned. Instead, doubt clouded her vision.

The week passed so slowly, Connie didn't think she would see the end of it. When she miscalculated a refund to a customer who came storming back, asking her if she had taken math in high school, Connie thought she was about to lose it. The precious peace she had tried to hang onto was gone. Even prayers were hard to offer up anymore.

"What's the matter?" Donna finally asked. "You aren't yourself at all."

"Lance flew the coop."

"Huh? What are you talking about?"

"He's been gone a week and didn't even tell me he was leaving. He never called either. His grandfather said he had gone home. For all I know, his family talked him out of our relationship. The curse that affected Gene and Bette has happened once again."

"Honey, you'd better stop with these wild ideas of yours. You know Lance is crazy about you."

"If he was, then don't you think he would have told me what he's doing? Maybe he's gone off to see another woman."

"Connie, you know better than that. You had brothers. Did they ever tell your mother where they were going?"

"Hardly ever." Louis and Henry were very bad at alerting the family of their whereabouts, nor did they ever remember the telephone for notifying the family. Many nights Mom waited up late, wondering if they would walk through the door alive. She would scold them for not finding the phone booth to call, even after giving them money. These days she would have given them a cell phone, but that didn't always work either as Connie discovered with Lance.

"That's men for you. They tend to be a little preoccupied at times. So just be patient. You know the saying. Absence makes the heart grow fonder."

For Connie, Lance's stark absence only lent itself to more strange stories and scenarios. When Saturday arrived, she decided to work some overtime, unwilling to spend the weekend at home wondering what Lance was up to. She again tried calling his place and still received no answer. She thought of trying his grandfather one more time, but he had seemed nonchalant about the whole venture as if there was nothing to worry about. *So stop worrying, Connie,* she told herself.

At church on Sunday she finally saw Lance scurry in late to the service. Instead of going to see her, he rushed forward to greet others in the congregation. Connie bit her lip. Salty tears burned her eyes. It was just as she feared. His family disapproved of her, and now it was over between them.

Connie didn't even wait for the service to conclude but headed straight for her car, brushing away the tears as she went. She didn't intend to make a spectacle of herself in front of everyone in church. She opened the car door, preparing to leave, only to find a gift-wrapped box sitting on the driver's seat.

"What is this. . . ?" she began. Her hands trembled. She sat down in the driver's seat and began fumbling with the wrapper. Inside was a brand-new cuckoo clock, exactly like the one that once hung in Grandma's house—the instrument that once imparted so much comfort then and now. On a whim, she turned the clock over and found a small box taped to the back. "What is this. . . ?" she said again.

Just then a familiar hand touched hers through the open door of the car. She trembled, knowing at once the presence and the scent of cologne. Lance.

"Let me get that for you." He moved around to the other side of the car and slid into the passenger seat.

Connie didn't know what to say. Everything became a blur. When he untaped the small box and gave it to her, the tears flowed freely down her face.

"Connie," he began, concerned by her reaction.

"I thought they talked you out of it," she moaned, opening the box to reveal a beautiful diamond ring. "I thought your family would tell you to go find someone rich."

"I did find someone rich. Connie Ortiz. Rich in mercy, rich in compassion, rich in love. I know this isn't exactly the greatest place to ask for your hand, here in your car. Maybe we can go somewhere quiet."

"This is perfect. And the answer is yes!" She slipped the ring onto her finger.

He smiled. "I hope you weren't totally put out when I didn't tell you my plans. As you can see, I was on a secret mission. Granddad said you'd called."

"I must admit, I wasn't sure what to think."

"Now you know. By the way, I did see my family. All my sisters want to plan the wedding, from the shower down to the reception. So you're covered."

"They really want me to be a part of the family?"

"Of course they do. They would like to meet you as soon as possible. After I got done sharing with them what's happened these last few weeks, there wasn't a dry eye in the house. Connie, you made a great impression. But most important of all, you made an impression on me." He leaned over to kiss her.

Instead, Connie stood the clock up, adjusted the settings, and pulled the chain all the way to the floor of the car. The bird appeared with its first greeting.

Lance jumped at the sound. He looked at Connie and laughed. "What was that all about?"

"Don't you know? Time's up!" She set down the clock and fell into his tender embrace.

A Letter To Our Readers

Dear Reader:

In order that we might better contribute to your reading enjoyment, we would appreciate your taking a few minutes to respond to the following questions. We welcome your comments and read each form and letter we receive. When completed, please return to the following:

Fiction Editor
Heartsong Presents
PO Box 719
Uhrichsville, Ohio 44683

1. Did you enjoy reading *Time Will Tell* by Lauralee Bliss?
   ❏ Very much! I would like to see more books by this author!
   ❏ Moderately. I would have enjoyed it more if

   _____
   _____
   _____

2. Are you a member of **Heartsong Presents**?   ❏ Yes ❏ No
   If no, where did you purchase this book? _____

   _____

3. How would you rate, on a scale from 1 (poor) to 5 (superior), the cover design? _____

4. On a scale from 1 (poor) to 10 (superior), please rate the following elements.

   ____ Heroine   ____ Plot
   ____ Hero   ____ Inspirational theme
   ____ Setting   ____ Secondary characters

5. These characters were special because?_____
_____
_____

6. How has this book inspired your life?_____
_____
_____

7. What settings would you like to see covered in future
   Heartsong Presents books? _____
_____
_____

8. What are some inspirational themes you would like to see
   treated in future books? _____
_____
_____

9. Would you be interested in reading other **Heartsong
   Presents** titles? ❏ Yes ❏ No

10. Please check your age range:
    ❏ Under 18   ❏ 18-24
    ❏ 25-34   ❏ 35-45
    ❏ 46-55   ❏ Over 55

Name_____
Occupation _____
Address _____
City_____ State_____ Zip_____

Sweet Treats

4 stories in 1

*T*hese four complete novels follow the culinary adventures—and misadventures—of Cynthia and three of her culinary students who want to stir up a little romance.

Four seasoned authors blend their skills in this delightful compilation: Wanda E. Brunstetter, Birdie L. Etchison, Pamela Griffin, and Tamela Hancock Murray.

Contemporary, paperback, 368 pages, 5 ³/₁₆" x 8"

♥ ♥ ♥ ♥ ♥ ♥ ♥ ♥ ♥ ♥ ♥ ♥ ♥ ♥ ♥

♥ ♥ ♥ ♥ ♥ ♥ ♥ ♥ ♥ ♥ ♥ ♥ ♥ ♥ ♥ ♥

-------- Presents --------